CHRISTMAS, CRIMINALS, AND CAMPERS

A Camper And Criminals Cozy Mystery

Book Four

BY
TONYA KAPPES

TONYA KAPPES
WEEKLY NEWSLETTER

Want a behind-the-scenes journey of me as a writer? The ups and downs, new deals, book sales, giveaways and more? I share it all!

As a special thank you for joining, you'll get an exclusive copy of my cross-over short story, *A CHARMING BLEND*. Go to Tonyakappes.com and click on subscribe in the upper right corner to join.

CHRISTMAS, CRIMINALS, AND CAMPERS

The loudest scream I've ever heard came from the office.

I stood there in slow motion as I watched Hank draw the gun from the hidden holster under his shirt. I shoved past him, running towards the office. It was as though my feet had a mind of their own.

"Abby?" I questioned when I got to the door and noticed she was standing over Nadine White on the floor. "Did you scream?"

I could feel Hank behind me.

"Abby?" Hank called.

She stood with her back to us. My eyes drew down her body until they saw the bloody knife dangling from her fingers.

She turned around. Her eyes hollow.

"She's dead," she replied in a small frightened voice.

CHAPTER ONE

"The way Nadine carefully wove the tapestry of the small town really did make it feel like its own character," Abby Fawn said with a deep sigh of happiness. She spoke so fondly of the book she had picked for The Laundry Club's monthly book club meeting.

It was no secret that Abby Fawn was Nadine White's biggest fan. Many times, Abby used her position as a librarian to get advance reading copies of Nadine's books before they were published.

"No matter what we say about the book, Abby is going to defend it until she convinces us to feel the same way." Dottie Swaggert curled her nose as though she smelled dirty laundry a tourist was throwing into the closest washing machine.

The Laundry Club was a full-service laundromat in downtown Normal, Kentucky. It wasn't just a place to do your laundry; it was like nothing you've ever seen. It was upscale, and Betts Hager had done a fabulous job making it feel like the comforts of home for the customers.

Since Normal was located smack dab in the middle of Daniel Boone National Park, it was a tourist destination for campers and hikers who needed a laundry facility. Betts wanted her customers to be as comfortable doing laundry at The Laundry Club as they were in their homes. She set up a coffee and drink bar and offered snacks. She had a sitting area complete with a television and couches. The customers loved to hang around the puzzle area where there was always a jigsaw puzzle to solve. The little library area, where we held our monthly book clubs, had shelves stocked with books from Abby that the library could no longer use or were too damaged to put on the shelf as well as a computer.

It was the first place I'd come to do my laundry when I drove into Normal in my camper. And here is where I'd met these ladies that I now could rely on for anything I ever needed. We'd truly become what the name was - The Laundry Club.

"Do you have something to say about *Cozy Romance in Christmas?*" Abby directed her question to Dottie.

"Nope." Dottie sat back, crossing her arms in front of her. "I thought it could've used a little more oomph if you know what I mean."

"This is a very popular women's fiction book. It was my pick and I wanted to pick something that gave us a good and happy feeling inside that we can hold onto during the Christmas season since our next book club won't be until the new year." Abby jerked her head towards me. Her brown-haired ponytail whipped around her. "Mae? What are your thoughts on the town being its own character?"

"Well." I hesitated by taking a moment to look at the front of the book to get the author's name.

We all knew that Dottie liked her novels a little steamier and Queenie French liked her cowboy romances, but honestly, I preferred a good cozy mystery. Over the past few months I'd even used some tricks I'd learned from my favorite cozy mystery authors to help the local sheriff's department bring a few criminals to justice.

"Um. . . Nadine White does make you feel like you are in the town on the cover." I held the book up with the cover facing outwards. "I love how the snow is falling in front of the yarn shop. It's also cute how the cat is in the display window."

"But what about the friendships Nadine wrote about in the novel?" Abby asked.

"If y'all treated me with kid gloves and all the rah-rah we are sisters stuff, I'd think you'd lost your ever-lovin' mind." Dottie didn't waste any time giving her opinion.

"I think it was very nice." Betts Hager was opening The Laundry Club's mail. "No matter what you think, Dottie, our little group has become a much-needed girls' group for me just like Nadine created in the book. There were some people with flaws, but it's fiction." She ripped open an envelope and pulled out a letter. "What about you, Queenie?" Betts asked another member of our book club, pushing back a strand of her wavy shoulder length hair and brushing her bangs to the side as she read the letter to herself.

"I'm not saying it was the worst book we've read, but I'm certainly not going to continue with the series." Queenie adjusted the Jazzercise logo headband up over her forehead. Her short blonde hair was sticking straight up like a bunch of matchsticks. She did look great for being in her sixties, but her colorful wardrobe choices could use a little improvement. "There's like twenty books in the series."

Abby Fawn's brows drew down.

"Abby, we all liked it, but just not as much as you." I reached over to give her comfort.

"Guys," Betts Hager put her hands in her lap, gripping the letter. "We all better really like it because Nadine White is coming to our book club."

"What?" Dottie's face pinched.

Abby reached across our circle of chairs and snatched the letter out of Betts's hands.

"I always invite the authors we pick to The Laundry Club book club meetings, never figuring one would show up."

"Oh my Gawd!" Abby shook with excitement. "She's getting ready to write her next novel over the winter and will be in Normal for Christmas. When she looked up Normal on the internet, she noticed all of my social media posts and hashtags. She decided that she's going to check out Happy Trails Campground and rent a camper for the entire winter season to work on her next novel."

"Happy Trails?" That got my attention right away since I was the owner of the tourist destination of choice deep in the Daniel Boone National Park.

Long story short, my now-dead ex-husband had gone to jail for a Ponzi scheme after swindling millions of dollars from people all over the country, including all the women in the book club. When he went to jail, I had no idea he'd named me the owner of a rundown campground while everything else was seized by the government.

Going from the high life in Manhattan to a campground in Normal wasn't my idea of fun or the way I had wanted to spend my life. I'd spent the better part of my teenage years getting out of the Kentucky foster care system after my own family had been killed in a housefire.

It had taken me a few months to get the campground up and running on top of doing many odd jobs around the quaint town of Normal, but I'd made it a success. In doing so, not only did I gain the trust of the citizens that my husband had abused, but I had also brought the tourists back to the sleepy town by offering luxurious camper-style arrangements that were better than any hotel in Daniel Boone National Park.

Over the past couple of seasons, Happy Trails Campground had been used for family reunions, honeymoons, and family outings. I was proud of what I had done and its impact on our small town, and Abby Fawn had worked alongside me by doing her fabulous social media marketing in addition to being the town's librarian.

"I ain't never gotten no call about a Nadine White." Dottie Swaggert reached out to get the letter from Abby. She would know. She and I both lived at the campground. She was the manager and took all the reservations.

"Can I have that letter to keep?" Abby gushed with delight and took her phone out of her pocket. "Hashtag Nadine White is going to join the hashtag The Laundry Club hashtag book club to talk about her hashtag women's fiction hashtag novel hashtag *Cozy Romance in Christmas*."

"Abby!" Betts called out her name when she realized Abby was plastering Nadine White's visit all over social media.

"What was that?" I looked around when the lights in the laundromat flickered.

"The snow." Betts waved it off. "We have overhead powerlines out back that feed the electric and the heavy snow will sit on the line, wreaking havoc with the electricity." She pointed to the television that showed a snowy picture instead of the Weather Channel we had been watching on because there was a snowstorm headed our way. "The electricity rarely goes out, but the internet and cable do. Abby," she got Abby to look up from her phone. "You can't put it on social media. In her letter, she specifically states that it's a getaway and no one but her agent will know where she is."

"Oh, no." Abby clicked and swiped away on her phone. "I don't have service."

"You better get service fast because she's coming today." Dottie shoved the letter in my face.

"Today?" My jaw dropped. "I didn't have her reservation."

"Not under her name, but under Valerie Young." Dottie poked at the paper with her finger. "That's her agent."

"Valerie Young is the one who requested a Christmas tree and some fun lights around the rental camper." I had just finished putting up the Christmas tree last night in anticipation of her arrival.

"You've got to do more than that," Abby's voice rose with each word as the joy and anticipation over her favorite author's arrival bubbled up within her. "You've got to go all out and decorate the outside too."

"I did see Buck put some new decorations in the display window of the Tough Nickel Thrift Shop." Queenie unzipped the fanny pack that was clasped around her waist and took out an emery board to file a hangnail.

"You've got to do it. Can't you tell how much that Nadine loves Christmas from this book?" Abby begged. "I can help. I've read all of her books and there's a few Christmas ones. She loves tree all decorated in colored bulbs and she loves those snowmen blow ups. Loves them," she emphasized with her hands along with wide open eyes. "I've got to invite her to the library to do a reading." Abby jumped up and started to pace. She'd stop, hold her phone up in the air, look at it, shake it, and do it all over again in an effort to get some cell service. "It's perfect. A Christmas present for Normal."

"I'm not so sure she wants anyone to know she's here." Betts sighed. We all stared at Abby in amazement. She was so giddy and childlike. Granted, she was in her early twenties and the youngest of the group, but it was an author, not some big Hollywood actress.

"No." I put my hand out. That was the last thing she needed to be involved in. I'd never seen Abby this excited, not even since she'd started dating Ty Randal, one of Normal's most eligible bachelors and kinda a suitor of mine when I first moved to Normal. "You've got a lot on your mind and I'm crunched for time to get the camper ready."

"It's her own fault if she didn't tell you to get more decorations ups." Dottie tugged her cigarette case out of her front pocket. "Come on, I'll go with ya."

"So it's set." Abby gathered in the middle of us before we all went our separate ways. "If I can get Nadine White to do a book reading at the library, you're all coming, right?"

"Can I tell her that her book is no good?" Dottie took out a cigarette, sticking it in the corner of her mouth and letting it bounce as she talked. "She needs to be told that she needs more substance than a romantic fling and hoping to find love again."

"Dottie, I promise. You are going to love her. She's amazing." Abby's smile was brighter than the North Star on the night Jesus was birthed. Well, at least brighter than how I pictured it. "I have to go! I've got to get to some internet and take down that tweet about her being here."

The rest of us stood there watching Abby bolt out the door into the falling snow, leaving her coat on the back of her chair.

"Poor girl." Queenie tsked, clasped her hands, and bended forward to the ground. "I guess I better get to the church. I've got a Jazzercise class to teach and that undercroft gets really cold if they haven't put the heat on."

Queenie gave hugs all around.

"We've got the heat on." Betts moved the chairs from the circle back to where they belonged. "I made sure Lester knew." Lester was Betts's husband and preacher of the Normal Baptist Church.

"The three of you aren't getting no younger, so you better come join me for some good cardio exercise." Queenie wiggled her fingers into jazz hands before she slipped her hot pink gloves over them.

"Here." Betts had run over to the coffee bar and made to-go cups of coffee. "Take a cup with you. It's cold out there."

Betts was a woman who wore many hats. She not only did everything she could to be a wonderful wife and mother, she ran The Laundry Club, which was doing great, cleaned houses on the side, and was involved with various clubs around town.

Dottie and I said our goodbyes to Betts and put our coats on.

"I sure hope Abby doesn't get her hopes up." Dottie stood on the sidewalk and lit her cigarette.

"I'm worried about that too. She's built her up in her mind to be this wonderful woman. I just hope Nadine White doesn't disappoint her number one fan." I wrapped my hand around the crook of Dottie's arm. "Let's walk on over to the thrift shop and see what decorationsBuck's got over there for Nadine's camper."

CHAPTER TWO

Downtown Normal was truly beautiful in falling snow. I had never lived here before during the winter and the scenery didn't disappoint. In Kentucky, we had all four seasons. I'd have to say that fall happened to be one of my favorites, with all the changing colors Mother Nature offered deep inside the forests of Daniel Boone National Park.

The shops downtown were all different shapes and sizes. Some were cute chippy buildings and some were quite large, but none of them had big signs. They all had small, wooden, hand painted signs. There was The Smelly Dog Groomer, Cookie Crumble Bakery, Normal Diner, the Normal Library, Sweet Smell Flower Shop, The Trails Coffee Shop, Grassel's Gas Station, Deter's Feed-N-Seed, and the Tough Nickel Thrift Shop, to name a few.

"It looks like Abby has gone into Sweet Smell." Dottie drew her finger along Abby's footsteps in the snow and pointed into the window of the flower shop as we passed by.

"She is probably telling them all about Nadine White." I shook my head and looked both ways before Dottie and I crossed the one-way street along that side of the median to cross to the other side of Main Street.

Main Street was split in two, right down the middle. One-way streets on each side. In the middle was a small amphitheater, covered shelter, and several picnic tables scattered around the tall trees. During the warmer seasons, it was a wonderful place to have lunch while visiting downtown or to see plays put on by the community theater. A lot of tourists liked to come down here and have family reunions in the shelter. In the winter, it was turned into a tree lot, with twinkling Christmas lights scattered around the perimeter of the entire area.

There were a few vendors and local artists set up that were allowed to sell what they made. Crafts were a big thing around here, especially anything monogrammed. It was definitely a great place to Christmas shop for someone because you were guaranteed to find something unique.

Dottie snuffed out her cigarette as we hurried across the streets and into the Thrifty Nickel. It was a neat shop owned by Buck. He'd left the old building exactly the way it was built, leaving the exposed brick on all the walls and the entire store open with tall ceilings. There was an upstairs full of clothing and a back room with thrift store items, but I was more interested in the blow-up snowman he'd displayed in the front window.

Dottie and I made sure to shake the snow off our coats and boats near the door. We didn't want to get Buck's hardwood floors or his oriental rugs wet. While she moseyed around to look at the big antique furniture and expensive items, I checked out all the Christmas things he had until I found Buck to ask about the snowman.

Buck was tall and slender with coal black hair. He was in his late sixties and was very knowledgeable about the history of not only Normal, but of all the items in his shop.

"Mae West. How's your first Christmas season in Normal?" Buck trotted down the steps. He had a stack of long johns in his hands.

"Surprising." It was a word I'd found myself using a lot when people asked about Happy Trails for the last couple of weeks. "I never figured anyone would want to stay at a campground during winter. Especially with the big snowstorms we are projected to get."

He folded and stacked the long johns into a tobacco basket he used for display near the front of the shop.

"I think it's that people love to gather and enjoy each other. At least, I hope that's what the campground offers. Which brings me to why I'm here." I gestured over to the snowman. "I have a special camper coming.."

"That writer woman?" He asked, interrupting me. I guess the look on my face asked him how he knew. "Abby came in here like a jumping bean she's so excited. Looking for a perfect gift for the woman. I had an old leather-bound book that she's going to turn into some sort of flower vase. She mumbled about going on over to Sweet Smell Flower Shop to get this woman's favorite flowers or something."

"Oh, boy." Abby was further gone than I had thought. "Abby is her biggest fan."

"I gathered that." He adjusted the pile of long johns and rubbed his hands together. "What about the snowman?"

"According to Abby, Nadine White - that's the author - loves blow up snowmen. I was wondering if I could either buy it or rent it from you to put in front of the camper she's staying in over the Christmas holiday." I had to admit it was super cute.

It wasn't too big or too small. It'd be perfect for the size camper she was renting.

"I also need some lights to go on the outside along with one of those multi-colored camper flag banners you sell." I might as well go all out just like Abby said Nadine would love. "I do want to show her the hospitality Happy Trials and Normal have to offer. Maybe she'll set her next book in a town like ours." I fluttered my lashes, knowing Buck was a sucker for a southern gal.

My insides began to flutter. Was I climbing aboard Abby's wagon and getting a little excited too?

"Oh, alright." He shook a finger at me. "Just because I like you, Mae West."

I stood near the window watching Buck make his way into the winter wonderland display he'd made. The snowman wasn't easy to get out of the window, but Buck forged ahead. I heard the snowman's fan turn off, followed by the sound of the round, white guy deflating.

The knock on the glass made me jump and look up. Bobby Ray Bond, my foster brother from when I was a kid who'd recently found me back in Normal, was waving from the sidewalk. He was dressed in a pair of thick mechanic's overalls, a knit blue cap, and a pair of snow boots.

I waved him in.

"May-bell-ine, what on earth are you doing out in this weather?" He scolded me, raking off his cap. What was left of his thinning, brown hair stuck up due to the static electricity from the hat. His brown eyes bore into me. "I don't think it's fittin' for you to be out when there's a storm coming."

"I'm fine, Bobby Ray. I lived through all the people milling about New York City all those years. A little snow isn't going to bother me." I reminded him that he was no longer my protector even though he was the one who'd paid for me to get out of Kentucky the minute I turned eighteen.

I mean the exact minute after, which was in the middle of the night. He'd given me enough money to get me to New York and I'd made all the arrangements. I hadn't looked back either. At least not until my ex and all that mess and his leaving me with the campground. It turned out to be a blessing in disguise. I'd actually found myself in love with being back in Kentucky.

I can't say I was exactly thrilled when Bobby Ray showed up at Happy Trails looking for a job and a place to live, only because I didn't want to relive my past. It was in the past and I didn't like to live there. Bobby Ray had embraced the new me and I'd felt like we'd moved past the foster family days.

"Okay. If you say so. I've got to get back to work." He slipped his hat back on his head. "I'll see you, Buck," Bobby Ray called out before he headed out the door and walked down Main Street towards Grassel's Gas Station where he worked.

Bobby Ray was a great mechanic and it was just his luck that Joel

Grassel had been looking for a good mechanic. I told him to look no further than Bobby Ray. He was the finest around. In Normal everybody brought their cars to him and he'd done right well for himself. He even bought the camper he'd been renting from me and was a full-time resident there along with me, Dottie, and Henry, my maintenance man. Other than that, the rest of the campers were intended to be rented for short periods of time. There were some bungalows nestled in the back of the campground, only they didn't have heat, so those weren't rentable for the winter.

"Here you go." Buck handed me the snowman all neatly folded like he'd done the stack of long johns. The blower for the snowman, a box of outside lights, and the banner were all stacked on top of the deflated snowman. " You just need to plug it in. The amps on the camper should be fine. It doesn't take up too much electricity."

He was talking about all the hookups and electricity required for the campers. Some of them required more since they were bigger and had more electric items, but the one Nadine's agent had rented was a simple camper with not many amenities.

"You're the best, Buck." I took the snowman. "I can have it back to you after the New Year."

"Nah, you keep it. But I do want to come to the campground's Christmas feast." He smiled. "I've got nowhere to be, so I figured I'd just show up there."

"You got it. We've got some good food planned." Each month I had a themed party at the campground.

It was originally for the campers' enjoyment, but they had gotten bigger and bigger since the citizens of Normal had gotten involved and I'd invited them. Happy Trials had needed a lot of work when I moved here. It was broken and rundown. Nothing worked. With the help of many of the local businesses and donations, we were able to get it up and running again. There was a year long wait for a reservation now.

We were booked solid for the month of December, and I knew the Normal Diner would be closed on Christmas Day. It was the perfect time to host a Christmas Day lunch for anyone who wanted to come, but with the impending weather, I was just hoping we would have electricity.

"Did you see Dottie upstairs?" I asked Buck, wondering where she'd disappeared to.

"Yep. She was trying on some new clothes I just received from an estate sale. I haven't even gone through all of it yet. But she helped herself," he said right before she appeared at the top of the steps.

"How much?" She had a plastic bag full of pink sponge curlers.

"Free. I don't think anyone wants used hair curlers but you." He laughed, shook his head, and pushed his hands down into the front pocket of his jeans. "I swear, Dottie Swaggert."

"Let's get out of here before the snow really starts to fall and we can't get this snowman up in time." I was more worried about getting the decorations up in time than the snow. "But first, I'm going to grab a small tree from the tree lot."

I'd bought a small Ford to get me around since I'd parked my RV at Happy Trails. It was sorta a pain in the neck to move once you got situated. I had to take everything down, put it away, and secure it in order to drive it, so when Joel Grassel had a car I could buy, I jumped at the chance. I had a golf cart to use around the campground, but not in the snow.

The little Christmas fir we picked out for the outside of Nadine's camper fit perfectly on top of the Ford.

There weren't many big highways around Normal. We were located in the middle of Daniel Boone National Park and Forest, which meant the roads were maintained by the county. This was a good thing since the National Guard was in charge and they kept the roads clear as best they could.

"It sure is coming down, Mae." Dottie drummed her fingers along the door. "You be careful."

"Don't you worry. I'll get you back in no time to get those new curlers in your hair." I joked, but kept my hands steady on the wheel. One slick spot and we'd no doubt hit a tree. "It looks like they're going to have to make a few passes on this road."

I looked in the rearview mirror at the snow covering my tire tracks faster than my wheels could make them.

Dottie reached over and turned on the radio. The latest weather update was just coming on.

"The Bluegrass Airport is going to be shutting down in two hours. If you are coming to the airport, be sure to check the status on any and all flights leaving out of or flying into the airport," the woman said. "The snow is falling at a more rapid pace than we'd initially anticipated."

I took it slow as I turned right into the campground's entrance and under the Happy Trails Campground sign. The entrance was a long and windy gravel road that took you deeper into the park before you entered the clearing where the cute and cozy campground was located.

"I wonder if our famous camper will be here?" Dottie asked a good question. She'd put her hands in her pocket and pulled out her cigarette case. "I'll be happy to get in my house."

"Did I make you nervous?" I laughed and drove further into the campground, passing the office building on the left and the storage units on the right before turning right onto the road that circled around the lake in the middle.

"You don't make me nervous." She had her door open before I could even stop the car in front of her camper. "This weather makes me cranky and achy."

"Alright. Be on the lookout for our famous guest," I told her. "Also, can you send a call out to Henry to meet me down at her camper, so I can get some help putting all this up?"

"Sure will!" She hollered and looked up at the sky. The snow was really coming down now. "You better hurry up or you're going to turn into a snowman."

CHAPTER THREE

The campground was surrounded by the park, with its wooded tree lines and entrances to many trails for different levels of hiking expertise. Each trail had something special to offer. The tall evergreens were as pretty as a picture with the snow caked on top of each branch and a burst of green popping out.

Happy Trails added to the park's natural beauty with lights around the campers and on all the trees that surrounded the lake. Henry had taken it upon himself to put white lights around all the tree trunks, making the lake look like a winter wonderland. Ty Randal, one of the residents who lived at the campground full time, had donated ice skates in various sizes to the campground. Instead of closing the cute tiki hut bar next to the dock for winter, we turned it into a skate shack, where guests could borrow skates and enjoy the frozen lake.

Instead of going to the right of the lake, I drove around the circle on the left, so I could drop off the Christmas tree. The rest of the stuff I'd bring over after I parked my car at my RV.

You could spot my RV from a mile away. The vibrant yellow pop top's awning was up with a farm-style picnic table underneath. I'd hung icicle lights around the awning and the camper. I loved Christmas and spending it here was perfect.

I parked the car on the concrete pad next to my RV.

The yelping from inside the RV came from Fifi, the miniature poodle I'd acquired from a woman's whose house I'd cleaned. Long story short, she was one of the suspects in a crime I'd helped solve. Only she'd gone to jail for a few days before I solved it and she picked me of all people to babysit her prized, award-winning poodle.

Unfortunately, it was during the summer and our busiest season. I let Fifi run around during one of the campground parties and Ethel Biddle's brown and white pug, Rosco, was seen in an uncompromising position with Fifi. And Fifi got pregnant. She'd done "gone to the wrong side of the tracks" as her original owner had told me and Fifi was no longer worth half a cent, making Fifi useless to her and my problem from then on.

"Hi, baby girl." I opened the door, greeted by a small ball of fur, tap dancing around on her four little paws. "You are exactly what I needed to see."

I picked her up and gave her a few kisses before sliding her paws into little shoes. It was ridiculous. Me with a dog. I'd barely been able to take care of myself, much less a dog. It'd been an adjustment for me to to stop by the RV to let her out or take her with me, which I'd been doing a lot. She didn't like the snow and the only way I could get her outside to do her business was to put these dog booties on her.

I'm sure they'd look adorable if I'd continued to keep her groomed like she'd been used to, with balls of fur in various places along her otherwise shaved body, but I couldn't do that to her in the cold winter. She shivered as it was, with a coat on. Besides, she didn't need to perform for anyone now that she owned me. And that's what it was. She owned me now.

"Want to come with me to decorate?" I asked Fifi once I'd put her down under the awning, so she'd get her footing and realize she was going to have to go potty in the snow. "I've got to put up a snowman and some lights."

I glanced across the lake at the mini camper Nadine had rented before I retrieved the wagon from the backside of the RV. It was one of those industrial wagons with big wheels. It was perfect for when I wanted to go to the lake with blankets and beach things. It was also perfect for wheeling Fifi around and for doing some gardening around the campground, though Henry did most of it.

"You comin'?" The familiar voice called from the distance, though the echo off the mountains and trees made it sound like Henry was much closer. "Gettin' colder by the minute!"

"I'm coming!" I hollered, pulling the cart behind me. Fifi did her business and ran over as quick as her little legs would carry her before she stood on her back legs and clawed the air with her front legs for me to pick her up. "I'm going to grab you a blanket too."

I talked to her like a person. I swear she knew what I was saying. It made me feel better to think she did. I carried her until we got to the car. After I put the items Buck had given me in the wagon, I grabbed a blanket from my backseat and put it in there with Fifi perched on top.

"Dashing through the snow, in a little wagon," I began to sing on our way over to the other side of the lake where Henry had started to put up a small Christmas tree. "Fififi, Fififi, Fifi all the way." I changed the lyrics to get my little pup to wag her cute tail when I said her name.

No matter what, she was always happy to see me, and it lifted my spirits.

"This here sure is a cute tree." Henry stood back from the little four-footer and went back to straighten it up. "Is this for your foster mama?"

I jerked up from the taking the blowup snowman out of the wagon.

"What did you say?" I was sure the bitter cold had frozen my eardrums. "I thought you said something about my foster mama." I laughed and turned back to get the electric fan to blow the lawn ornament up.

"I did." Henry had picked up the lights he'd gotten from seasonal storage unit and walked around the tree, placing them on the branches. "Bobby Ray said something about your foster mama comin' to visit or something."

I thought back long and hard to when I saw Bobby Ray at the thrift shop and he never mentioned Mary Elizabeth Moberly name once. Or trust me, I'da come unglued.

"Mae?" Henry called my name. It was like I was frozen right there in my snow boots. "Mae?"

I blinked a few times. The chill had left the outside of my body and moved inside to my organs.

"Did you say that Bobby Ray Bond," I said, pointing to Bobby Ray's camper, "said that?" I had to make sure I heard him correctly. "Because I know I'm not hearing you right."

"Yep. She's comin' for Christmas. He even asked Dottie if there was a rental available and when Dottie said we was all booked up, he mumbled about putting her in his camper or even up at one of the log cabins up on Tree Top Lookout."

"Or he could put her up in a cabin in Colorado," I groaned, knowing it was just like Bobby Ray to get a soft heart on me now. He was always a sucker around the holidays and if I knew Mary Elizabeth Moberly like I did, she was going to use that to her advantage.

"Colorado? Why Mae West," Henry cackled. "I'm not that smart on geography and all but I do believe that's clear out yonder across the United States."

"That's where she needs to be." My eyes narrowed as I glared across the lake wondering when it was the blizzard was going to blow in. And I didn't mean the snow blizzard.

THE DARKNESS during the winter months came much earlier in Daniel Boone National Park than it did other places in Kentucky. In most other parts of the state it got dark around six p.m. In the mountains of the park, it got dark around five p.m. and there wasn't much to do but sit in my RV staring across the lake to see when Nadine White was going to arrive.

Well...there was one thing I'd been doing that I'd tried not to do and that was stew over what Henry had said. I continued to tell myself I was waiting on Nadine White, but when Bobby Ray Bond's car rolled up next to his camper, I darted out the door.

"Well, well. May-bell-ine, you sure are in a rush to greet me from work. Are you inviting me to supper?" He smiled as big as the moon hanging over our head and as bright too. "It'll just take a second for me to clean up."

"Right now, the last thing I'm going to do is sit down for supper with you if what Henry told me is true." I stuck my hands in my coat pocket. The temperature had dropped at least ten degrees since the darkness had crept in and taken over any and all light.

"Do you mean that Henry didn't tell you I was visiting?" A familiar looking woman with glossy brown hair cut in a stylish way stood at the entrance of the camper. "Mae, you better get over here and give me some sugar."

There stood Mary Elizabeth Moberly in all her southern glory, pearls and all, with her arms outstretched. She was dressed head to toe in Lily Pulitzer or at least someone with a similar design. Trust me. I knew. She used to cover me in the same bright pinks and yellows.

"Whaaat?" Her southern voice dripped off her like the pearls around her neck. "You aren't happy to see me? I did take you in and give you a wonderful home after you bounced around to a few homes. Got you debutante lessons and etiquette classes and put you in the finest of clubs." She frowned, batted her eyes and jutted her arms out again. "I forgive you for not inviting me to your wedding. Though." Her head bobbled side-to-side. "I did hear it didn't end so gracefully." Her eyes raked over me.

Gracefully wasn't a word I'd used to describe the situation with my murdered ex-husband, but it was a word that Mary Elizabeth would use. And use often. It was that southern grace that she tried to put in me when I went to live with her and it was her southern manners that I fought against tooth and nail until I clawed my way out.

I found myself staring at that straight head of hair of hers that lay so perfectly over her shoulders. As I tried to tame down my curly hair by patting my head, I realized she was staring at my sweatshirt that had a picture of that Grumpy Cat from the internet. It was like a quarter from the thrift store and I thought it was cute.

I put my hands in my pocket and brought them to the middle of my stomach, forcing the jacket to close up around me. I would've zipped it up but didn't want to give her the satisfaction that I'd noticed she was judging me by my outfit. Sweatpants tucked in snow boots and a sweatshirt wasn't her idea of clothing, much less a sweatshirt with a big cat head and *Stay Away* printed across the front.

"Mae, she deserves to have Christmas with us now that you're back," Bobby Ray whispered as I continued to stare at Mary Elizabeth.

"Fine." I stomped. "But I won't call you mom," I protested and hurried back to my RV, where I was going to do what I did with every other situation that made me mad.

I would replay this over and over in my head until I'd ran over it with my car, dragged it home, and beaten it to death in my mind.

"Mae, honey, can't we just get along?" Her voice ran right through me, sending chills all along my spine.

In my head all I heard was "May-bell-ine, honey, you are a Moberly now. You need to act as if you have some good southern charm. That includes politeness, kindness, table manners, and social grace, all at the cost of happiness. Do you understand me, May-bell-ine? Are you listening to me, May-bell-ine? You can't get anything below an A in your classes. Don't you know that you've got to go the University of Kentucky and join my sorority? You can't be embarrassing me with mediocre grades. Do you understand your place in society, May-bell-ine?"

It was dialogue I'd replay in my head all night until I finally fell asleep and the alarm on my cell phone woke me the next morning.

CHAPTER FOUR

A light snow had fallen all night long. It was a nice powdery mix that swept away from the warm car tires along the pavement of the road around the campground instead of sticking and making everything slick as cat's guts. Henry had already used brine, a type of ice repellent, on the road to help out. Given the cost of our insurance, we had to make sure everything was safe and clear for all the campers in Happy Trails, including Mary Elizabeth.

The brewing of my much-needed coffee was a much-needed jolt to my foggy head. It was the smell that carried me out from underneath the warm covers and into the shower.

"Did Bobby Ray honestly think he was giving me a good Christmas by bringing her here? It's more like coal in my stocking and I was a very good girl this year. Okay, so the year didn't start out like I thought it was going to but still. Did he have to bring her here at Christmas?" I asked Fifi as I dumped some kibble in her bowl. "See, you know what I mean."

I took her wagging tail as confirmation that she agreed with me. Fifi gave me one last look before she started to devour the food. I poured myself a cup of coffee and watched out the window while I let my hair air dry a little before I decided what on earth I was going to wear. I had to work in the office this morning and later this afternoon I needed to head back into downtown to finalize all the merchant donations to Christmas Dinner at the Campground.

There was a rental car parked on the concrete pad next to Nadine's camper. The snowman was still blown up and all the lights were still on outside. That made me happy. They were there to greet her. She must've gotten in late because it took me a long time to fall asleep and I knew it was in the middle of the night before I'd finally given into my thoughts. I didn't hear a car drive into Happy Trails, which was unusual since at the top of the campground next to the office, the gravel usually spit up around tires, pinging things and creating all sorts of noises.

Then I turned my head towards Bobby Ray's camper. There was a light on like most mornings. Bobby Ray had to go to work and I wondered what on earth Mary Elizabeth was going to do with her time.

I shook my head, shaking any thoughts of her out of my head. I was a grown adult now and I needed to act that way. If she did try to correct me or mother me, I'd just have to stand my ground.

It took me longer than normal to get ready for work and get Fifi's little fake fur jacket on her.

"Did you drive up here?" Dottie Swaggert asked as soon as I opened the door to the office, Fifi wiggling around in my arms.

She never missed a beat. "What on earth do you have on? You got a fancy meeting or something?"

She asked, her eyes going up and down my body after I hung my coat up on the rack.

"Just coming to work." I bent down and put Fifi on the ground. She scurried over to Dottie knowing Dottie would give her a bite of her breakfast biscuit. "I've got to run into town this afternoon and make sure all the merchants are ready with their donations for Christmas Dinner at the Campground." I brushed down the front of my red pencil skirt before I unbuttoned the matching red suit jacket.

"Henry put up the rest of the flyers about the dinner around town."

She looked me up and down. "Everyone is excited about wearing an ugly Christmas sweater."

My red heels ticked across the tile floor of the office. Inwardly, I groaned with each step. I'd not worn heels since I'd stepped foot in the RV months ago. This was one of a few clothing items I'd brought with me or that my lawyer had packed and sent to the campground before I'd driven here.

"Well, if you ask me, that's suit's uglier than a pair of bowling shoes." Dottie's lips were pressed together in a hard line. "You can wear that outfit as your ugly Christmas sweater at the dinner."

"Did I ask you?" I sat down in my chair and let out a long sigh. "I want to look good for when I go see everyone about donations."

"Did you forget that you didn't look like that when you asked them? And your face? What did you do?" Dottie asked.

The sunlight coming through the windows must've caught my face perfect.

"I put on a mud mask last night and I fell asleep before I took it off." I'd tried to cover it over with make-up, but Dottie had better eyes than an eagle.

"You need to go back home and put on some winter clothes. It's coming and you're gonna slip, fall, and break your neck." She grabbed a file and brought it over to my desk. "This here is the agreement signed by Nadine White. I found it underneath the door this morning when I came in."

I took the file from her and opened it up.

"Do you want me to get you a cup of coffee? I don't want your feet to give out on you." Dottie headed over to the coffeemaker we kept in the office.

I didn't even have to answer her. She'd already poured me a cup and brought it over while I read over all the extras Nadine had checked.

"It's like she decided to come and didn't bring anything." I noticed she'd picked the breakfast package, the cleaning package, and the linen package. "Like she decided to just put her finger on a map and go."

I should recognize this behavior. It was how I decided to go to New York City when I turned eighteen.

There were some things that left me scrambling when I'd moved to Normal. I had no idea how to keep a camper or RV. I had no knowledge of the purple bag (the poop bag), the electrical hook-ups, the water hook-up, or all the supplies I would need. That's how I came up with the idea to sell packages. Sometimes it was easiest just to show up and pay extra for the packages, so you didn't have to worry about bringing so many things from home.

The sound of gravel made me look out the window before I saw the zooming car fly by the office.

"Who on earth is driving so fast?" Dottie rushed over to the door and swung it open.

"Well, excuse me," Mary Elizabeth gasped, drawing a gloved hand up to her chest as her face drew back in a look of surprise.

Fifi jumped up from the blanket on the floor, teeth showing and yipping.

"Excuse you." Dottie nodded and pushed past Mary Elizabeth to get a look at the car speeding away. "Who are you, Nanook of the North?"

Mary Elizabeth looked as if she were getting ready to go on an Alaskan expedition in a full-length mink coat and matching hat.

"Please, stop that . . . that . . ." Mary Elizabeth pointed a gloved finger at Fifi. Fifi jumped up and tried to grab the edges of the mink.

"Fifi." I clapped my hands and pointed to the small bed next to my desk.

Fifi gave an extra little growl, getting the last word in before listening to my command.

"Mary Elizabeth." I stood up. The two women were both very strong-headed, and this was not how I needed them to meet. "This is Dottie Swaggert, the manager of Happy Trails." I pointed to Mary Elizabeth. "This is . . ."

"Mae West's foster mama," Dottie finished my sentence and did a slow walk around Mary Elizabeth, taking in all there was to see. "Our Mae sure didn't tell us that she was fostered in a home full of money."

"I'm sure our sweet Mae," Mary Elizabeth's tone held sarcasm, "probably didn't tell you much about the home we provided for her."

"Just the fact she skipped town right after her eighteenth birthday." Dottie slid her eyes towards me. "No wonder you're dressed in that get-up," she referred to my suit.

"Get-up?" Mary Elizabeth scoffed. "As the manager, I believe you could learn a lesson or two from how Mae dresses. I did spend a lot of money on her modeling lessons, so she would take pride in herself."

Mary Elizabeth slowly unhooked the eye hooks that ran down the front of the fur and slipped it off as graceful and smooth as her southern accent.

"Here." She held it out to Dottie.

"I'll take it." I jumped up from the chair and grabbed it before Dottie could light a cigarette and put it out on it. "I hear you knew she was coming," I said to Dottie under my breath when I passed her to hang up the coat.

She grunted but didn't move her eyes from Mary Elizabeth.

"Would you like to join us for a cup of coffee?" I asked.

"Yes. Please, a straw if you have one." Mary Elizabeth pulled on the fingers of her gloves before she elegantly peeled them off her hands.

Dottie's mouth gaped open while Mary Elizabeth did the routine I knew all too well. Where she walked into a room and commanded it from the time the soles of her heels hit the floor. Mary Elizabeth had a style and ease that carried her around the room like a feather floating on the breeze until she found a seat in front of my desk. She swept her fingers along the top of my desk and took a good look at them before snarling at the dust.

"Thank you." She brushed the dust off her fingers and accepted the cup of coffee, taking the tiniest sip through the straw. She put the coffee cup on top of the desk and leaned over to look at Fifi.

Dottie's nose curled, making her mouth open even more. "Too bad she didn't lean too far," Dottie mumbled.

"Mary Elizabeth takes pride in how white her teeth are, so she drinks through a straw." It was another memory that I'd stuck in the back of my head along with the gloves she made me wear as a child.

"Oh, Mae." Mary Elizabeth tsked. "Dottie, I'm sure you'll understand. We gave Mae the finest. We hated that she came from the mudflat as a child and adopted her."

"Fostered me," I corrected her.

"We legally adopted her," Mary Elizabeth said matter of factly. "After we adopted her, we put her in the best private schools."

"You sent me off to a boarding school." It was so funny how her recollection of my life was completely different than the one I had lived and will never forgive her for.

"It was an all-girls' prep school. She was going to attend the finest college and make something of herself." Mary Elizabeth glanced around the room.

"I'm thinking her owning a campground wasn't in your plan." Dottie was one that saw it and said it. She didn't mince words. You always knew where you stood with her.

"It sure wasn't. But no sense in looking backwards when we have so much catching up to do." Mary Elizabeth put her hands in her lap. "Now, where do we go to get your hair fixed?"

"I've got a meeting." I had wondered how long it was going to take her to say something about my hair. When she'd sent me off to boarding school, she took me to a salon to have them fix me. They ended up burning my hair and I was ridiculed all year long. "Dottie, do you mind watching Fifi for me?"

I lost my parents and had been moved around to two different families over six months. Yes, Mary Elizabeth and her husband Jerry had adopted me. I'd protested in the courtroom, but the judge said that I needed a home and the Moberlys had always wanted a child of their own. It wasn't enough for them to have Bobby Ray Bond. He was a boy. Mary Elizabeth wanted a girl she could groom and play with. I was already a teenager whose parents let me go with my friends to public school and play soccer, not Barbies. We didn't have a lot of money, but my family's house had been filled with love. Something Mary Elizabeth thought came in the form of manners and learning how to talk properly.

When I didn't use the table manners I had learned at the country club, she'd throw a fit, saying I was rebelling against her and not appreciative of the money they were spending on me to get me educated.

"But I just got here." Mary Elizabeth drew her shoulders back. "I thought we could just talk."

"I'm sorry if Bobby Ray gave you the impression that I wanted to spend the holidays with you. No matter what you think..." I walked over to get my coat. "My life is great. My husband was a loving man to me until I found out the awful things he did to others. We had a nice life and yes, my world was torn apart a few months ago, leading me straight back to Kentucky." I laughed because I'd spent the better part of my life trying to forget my life here and move on. "Here, I have not only grown the economy in Normal." I pointed to the framed article on the wall where the National Parks Magazine had done a feature story on me and how much bringing Happy Trails back to life had also brought the economy back to our cozy town. "I gained true friends. Friends who don't care that I was poor growing up. Friends that don't care if I lick my fingers. Friends that don't care if I wear sweatpants."

"Actually, we don't want to see you lick your finger." Dottie gave a slight smile. "But we do love you. And I'd love to keep Fifi here with me."

"I have never in my life. . ." Mary Elizabeth stood up.

I didn't bother waiting to see what Mary Elizabeth had to say to me before I slammed the office door behind me.

CHAPTER FIVE

"I just don't know who she thinks she is." I stuffed a forkful of gravy and biscuits in my mouth. "Seriously, she thinks she can come here and act as if she was the best foster mother around?"

My phone chirped a text from Abby Fawn.

"I thought you just said she said she adopted you." Trudy leaned her hips against the counter of the Normal Diner. Her hand dangled the coffee pot, with her elbow tucked into the waist of her lanky, five-foot-eight-inch frame. The long, dishwater blonde ponytail pulled around her shoulder and down the yellow button-up diner dress.

"I'll never claim them. Never," I protested and took another bite, swiveling my body in the stool butted up to the counter. I hit the message button on my phone and quickly read through Abby's text. She'd gotten confirmation that Nadine would be at the library today at two p.m. to talk to The Laundry Club book club members about the book.

"Well, I think you look as pretty as a picture." She dragged the white coffee mug that had a small chip on the rim across the counter and refilled my coffee. "Better than this awful yellow thing the Randals are making us wear."

"Thank you. I guess I shouldn't get all crazy over just a visit." I gnawed on my lip. "She really can't do anything to me. I'm an adult."

"That's right. Just like Preacher Lester says, it's our attitude about things." She patted my hand and took off down the counter, refilling all the empty mugs along the way.

Even though I knew Trudy was right, I still didn't feel like listening to her. I wanted to be mad and feed my emotions with the awesome southern-style biscuits and gravy Ty Randal had made.

I quickly texted Abby back letting her know I'd be there. It's not that I didn't want to go, although I did have a lot of work to do on the Christmas Dinner at the Campground. It's just that I wasn't ready to be so easily available to Mary Elizabeth. I had to get a grip on feeling towards her like I did when I was a teenager. But I wasn't so sure what those feelings were. They were still just as confusing now as they were then. I'd been to several therapists the year I left Kentucky, but never truly felt like I'd gotten any sort of answers. I'd let the bitterness take hold of my heart and let it fester there for her.

The front door of the diner opened, sweeping in the frigid air and sending chills along my legs after the cold found my ankles.

"Aren't we all fancy today." Hank Sharp's green eyes twinkled. His black hair was perfectly combed to the side.

My heart quickened. I gulped down the bite of gravy and biscuits I'd just stuffed into my mouth. He reached his hand over to my mouth, placing his thumb under my chin and using his forefinger to gently touch the corner of my lip.

"You had a little gravy." He smiled seductively, or at least in my head it was, before he reached over my shoulder to grab a napkin from the steel napkin holder on the counter. His cologne carried past him and tickled my nose.

"I'll grab us a table." The woman tapped him on the shoulder.

"Is that…?" I pointed and reached for my purse that I'd put on the floor since I'd decided to sit at the stool. I pulled out Nadine White's book from book club and flipped it to the back where there was her bio and a photo. "That's Nadine White."

"Yes. It is." He nodded and reached around me, pinching off a piece of my biscuit.

"Stop that. I need some comfort food." I smacked his hand away, teasing him.

We had been doing this little flirting dance with each other over the past couple of months and had yet to take it to anything more than that. The closest thing to a date we have had was his popping by for a cup of coffee at my RV.

"What's going on?" He asked as if he weren't with Nadine.

"What's going on with you and Nadine?" I asked, leaning back to get a look at her.

"She said something about social media getting out that she was here and how there was this one photographer person who stalks her. Apparently," he let out a long sigh, "she's decided to live in Normal for the majority of the winter months and sorta hide out. She wants some confidence in the sheriff's department and forest rangers that her calls will be taken seriously if this guy does show up."

"Hmmm," I hummed, knowing it had to have been Abby's hashtags that had gotten the word out. "So you brought her to breakfast?"

"I told her to meet me here. And she just told me that she's staying at a campground called Happy Trails." He smiled so big like he had a secret.

"What?" I asked. "You're hiding something."

"She also said that when she got there, the place looked like the north pole. She said she's going to talk to the manager about taking some of the decorations down."

"Have you read these books of her?" I smacked him in the chest with it. "She loves Christmas in them. I just wanted her to feel welcome and at home."

I was going to kill Abby Fawn when I saw her next.

"And they really aren't that great." I shrugged, feeling a little jealous that he was having breakfast with her when he'd never invited me to eat out. The fact she was pretty didn't help matters either.

I mean. . . She had straight, shoulder length, brown hair with caramel highlights in the right places. She had a nice olive complexion with perfectly shaped lips. Her nose fit her face dead set in the middle while mine jutted slightly to the right at the tip. She also appeared to be stylish with a black overcoat neatly buttoned then tied at the tapered waist.

"I'm sure you know that I prefer a good dead body mystery over any friendship mushy stuff." I reminded him in a not so subtle way how I was the one who had helped him solve a few cases around here.

"Is she the reason that's got you all up in arms?" He asked.

It didn't go unnoticed that he looked at her. Their eyes met and he gave her the one more second finger gesture.

"No. Bobby Ray invited my foster mother. . ."

"Adopted mother," Trudy corrected me. "Two coffees?" she interrupted, asking Hank.

"Yes. Thank you." He nodded at her then looked back down at me. "Adopted?"

"Bobby Ray invited our foster mother to Christmas without telling me. She showed up last night." I picked up the coffee cup and took a drink.

"You know, we've never talked much about your past." His jaw tensed. He ran a hand through his black hair. "Maybe we can grab some supper or something. I've got a good ear."

"Hank Sharp, are you asking me out on a real date?" I asked, trying to stop the huge grin I felt creeping up on my face.

"I think I am, May-bell-ine West." He drew out my real name in his long, slow, southern drawl, making it sound so much cuter than it truly was. "What if I pick you up around six tonight?"

"That is perfect. It gives me time to go to the library where your new citizen for the winter is going to give a small talk to our book club group. Abby Fawn is a huge fan of Nadine's and giddy as a child on Christmas Eve."

"Great. I'll pick you up at six." He started to walk away, but turned back around. "Mae, please don't be the date that doesn't eat."

"Don't worry. I'm not." Now, a few years ago when I'd started to date my Paul West, my dead ex-husband, things were different. I was a flight attendant. I'd met him and became his private flight attendant, which quickly turned into a romantic relationship.

He swept me off my feet, lavishing me with gifts. Flying me all over the world, keeping me draped in the finer things in life. I loved the clothes, the handbags, and all the facials, not to mention the fine dining and trips. I'd realized I'd become exactly who Mary Elizabeth had dreamed I'd be, minus the college education.

Trust me, Mary Elizabeth never intended me to use a college education. She just expected me to find good breeding stock there. Life here in Normal seemed like the real me and maybe that's why I held such a grudge against Mary Elizabeth.

I needed to explore and dig deep to find out what it was I didn't like about her if I was ever going to get over it. It wasn't bothering her any. It was funny how it was bothering me and more and eating me alive inside.

Having Mary Elizabeth send me away to boarding school should have been enough, but the second year I was there, I'd put my foot down and started to defend myself and others against the rich girl bullies, making me the most popular kid there. Still, I hated it and I hated that my family had died, but like I always did when life served me lemons, I just kept going.

"Who is that?" Trudy lifted her chin towards Hank and Nadine.

"She's some big author. We read her book for book club. Abby loves her. She's staying at the campground for a couple of months. Apparently, she wanted to let the law know she's in town in case those trashy magazines hear of it and invade our little town."

"Really?" Trudy's brows rose. "I might have to pick up a book and see exactly what she writes."

"I'm sure you can come to the library today around two. She's going to meet with our book club and answer questions I guess." I picked up my coffee cup and brought it to my lips.

My eyes zeroed in on Nadine putting her hand on top of Hank's, flipping her hair as a giggle escaped her lips. Our eyes met, hers narrowing and mine popping open when I recognized her look.

"Ah oh." Trudy put the coffeepot on the counter and crossed her arms. "It appears she's wanting some company while she's visiting."

"Yeah. Right. Over my dead body," I groaned and looked away.

But not for long.

"What's going on out there?" Trudy nodded towards the window.

I turned my head to look over my shoulder and when I did, I caught a glimpse of horror on Nadine's face.

There were two women in the middle of the snowy median on Main Street. One of them had a camera strapped around her neck while the other one was pulling at it with her hands.

I felt a gust of wind along my back as Hank Sharp ran past me and out the front door of the diner. Like all good citizens who loved gossip and drama, the customers of the diner rushed out of the diner like stampeding cattle, all gawking and whispering about what on earth was going on.

Not me. I tapped my feet around on the base of the counter's footrest and swirled the stool so that my knees were facing Nadine White. It was just me, Nadine, Trudy, and the kitchen staff left in the diner. I didn't need to go see what was going on outside. It was cold and these heels weren't going to let me do it gracefully. I would just get Hank to tell me when we had our date that night.

"Hi, Nadine." I carefully stood up. Once I felt sure on my feet and looked a little less like a newborn giraffe, I picked up my coffee and headed her way. "May I?"

"I'm sorry. Do we know each other?" She asked.

"Actually, you're staying at Happy Trails Campground and I'm the owner. I'm the one who put up the ridiculous Christmas decorations that you found a little tacky." I sat down without her inviting me. "I have to apologize for that. Abby Fawn is the local librarian and my friend. You might recognize her name. She's a huge fan of yours and picked your book for our book club."

"Yes. I'm going to be visiting with you today." She nodded, putting on a much different expression than she worn earlier.

"Well, she's the one who has read all of your books. Probably five times over. But this Christmas book was the first book of yours I've read and apparently you write a lot about Christmas, making my friend Abby think you love and adore Christmas." I could tell she knew where this was going. "I understand that you hate the decorations, and I'm more than happy to take them down. I don't need you to be nice to me. I'm not in the market for a new friend while you're in town, but I will tell you that I won't have you being nasty to your number one fan while you're here."

I sucked in a deep breath when I noticed a young woman come through the diner doors. She glanced our way when she walked by, but her attention was focused on what was going on outside.

I heard her ask Trudy what was going on. Trudy leaned across the counter and whispered, causing the customer to look at me and Nadine.

"I'll make this fast because I've got to go back to work." I took a drink of my coffee. "Abby Fawn is one of the nicest people you'll ever meet. She takes pride in her job and the fact that she thinks she knows you. All I'm asking is that you don't burst her bubble by talking about the decorations. Trust me. I get it and I have thick skin, but Abby does not." I stood up and Nadine's eyes followed me. "If you can't show a little kindness while you're here, just stay in the camper. You'll find that everything you need is in there. If not, look across the lake at the camper with all the gaudy twinkling Christmas lights and the poodle with unruly hair - that's mine."

"Duly noted, Mae." Her face was stone.

The sound of customers filing back into the diner brought me out of the competitive staring contest Nadine and I seemed to be having, like we were at the grade school lunch table. At least, me and my friends used to see who could stare the longest without blinking. Make no bones about it, I was a champ every time, but today I decided it was best to go ahead and have peace instead of victory.

I took my seat back at the counter and let Trudy fill up my coffee cup one more time before I forced myself to go back to the campground. I'd been gone long enough to make it look like I'd been doing business like I said I had to do.

"What was that about?" I stopped Hank after he came back into the diner.

"Nadine was right. That was some sort of paparazzi and her agent. According to her agent, Nadine is writing her next book while she's vacationing here. It's highly anticipated and there's a big cash reward for anyone who can get a glimpse of what it's about."

"Romance, small town, friendships," I muttered. "All her books have that."

"Not this one. The agent told the photographer it isn't like anything Nadine has ever written before." He shrugged. "I don't know. I read Bait and Tackle." He smiled. "And keep the peace."

"Is that the photographer Nadine was worried about?" I asked, noticing over his shoulder that the agent and the photographer were still talking.

"Nope. Different one." He put his hands in his pockets. "I gotta get back to her and let her know that we aren't her security detail and how sorry I am that we can't keep a guy on her at all times."

"Yeah, sure." I smiled back.

"I am looking forward to tonight." He gave me a wink that sent my heart into palpitations.

"Did you say that's a famous author?" The customer who'd come in when I was talking to Nadine had sat down on the stool next to mine.

"Yes. Nadine White," I confirmed. I didn't care if everyone knew she was here. "Do you read?"

"I do. I write too." The young woman looked over her shoulder and watched as Hank and Nadine left.

"I don't know much about her, but I'm more than happy to extend an invitation to the library gathering today at two o'clock. She's going to speak to our book club and I'm sure one more won't hurt." I put some cash on the counter, but not before glancing back at Nadine White and my Hank Sharp.

Nadine had scribbled something on a piece of paper and folded it up. She smiled with a flirty look in her eye as she handed him the piece of paper. Their fingers met. My heart hurt.

CHAPTER SIX

The rest of the morning and through lunch was pretty quiet. After I went home to change into a pair of jeans and a sweater, Iwent to Nadine's camper and took down all the inside decorations, leaving her a note that I'd appreciate it if she could leave up the outside decorations just to appease Abby.

The agent must've been staying with Nadine because I saw them leave together when it was around the time I was leaving for the library.

"We are all full up. Do you understand, Henry?" Dottie questioned Henry since we had to leave someone in charge of the office during business hours so we could go to the book club.

"Yes. No vacancy." Henry nodded.

"Now, last time you said you understood, you double-booked some of the campers. So, tell me again what I said." Dottie jabbed her finger at him.

"No vacancy," he said again.

"What does that mean?" She asked him.

"He gets it." I turned to Henry. "If anyone calls, just take a message. Or you can let the machine get it. I just want you to answer any maintenance calls or hiking reports."

Hiking reports were from the rangers themselves. Since the snow had fallen and continued to fall, although lightly, they liked to update all open campgrounds on the conditions of the open hiking trails. Most trails were open, but the more rigorous trails usually closed for a couple of months in the winter since they consisted of thick forest and big drop offs.

"That I can do." He sat down at the desk and propped his feet up on the desk.

"Come on." I picked Fifi up and headed towards the door.

"Are you sure he can do it?" Dottie grumbled and groaned all the way to the car.

"He'll be fine." I opened the door to the back seat to put Fifi in her seatbelt. "What are you doing in here?"

Mary Elizabeth was perched up in the back like a bird in a nest.

"Oh, I invited her." Dottie had already situated herself in the front passenger seat.

"Yes. It was mighty nice of her too. She did inform me that I had to sit in the back." Mary Elizabeth's eyes focused on Fifi, then she looked at me. "That dog has better clothing than you."

"Okay." I put Fifi in Mary Elizabeth's lap.

"What am I supposed to do with this?" Her nose curled and she had a look of sheer terror in her eyes.

"You never let me have a dog. Now I've got one and if you want to be with me, then you have to be with her. You're bonding with and holding her because you are hooked in her seat belt." I couldn't help but smile looking at her all bunched up in a dog seat belt.

"I wondered why it was so small." She actually giggled and settled into the seat with Fifi on her lap.

It was apparent she wasn't going to enforce her no dogs ever policy and would suck it up.

I continued to give Dottie the death stare every so often because I wasn't sure where the friendship had started between her and mommy dearest, though that might've been a harsh word to use on Mary Elizabeth since she didn't beat me with wire hangers or anything else for that matter. She only tried to beat manners into me, though I felt I had been a pretty good kid considering the circumstances.

THERE WAS no place to park in front of the library or along Main Street.

"What on earth is going on?" The streets were jammed. I didn't see anything happening in the snowy median and I wasn't aware of a play being performed by the community playhouse.

"Who knows." Dottie shrugged and pulled out her cigarette case after I'd finally squeezed into a spot that may have put my Ford a teensy little bit over the yellow line on the curb. Before I could put the car in park, she'd jumped out and lit the cancer stick.

"You should tell her it's really bad for her health to smoke, not to mention her body odor." Mary Elizabeth waved a hand in front of her face for effect.

"Why don't you tell her?" I suggested, knowing how Dottie reacted to people when they told her that very thing. It's not like Mary Elizabeth would be the first one to tell her that.

"Hmm." Mary Elizabeth huffed and fumbled with the seat belt until she got it.

I took Fifi from her and carried her close to my body so she wouldn't get cold. The snow had started to come down in bigger flakes, but it was still the fluffier type that didn't leave the roads slick.

I let Fifi do a quick tinkle before we headed into the book club.

"Oh, my stars," Dottie gasped when we got to the door and saw it was standing room only inside of the library. "I've never seen more than two people in here and that includes Abby."

"Do you think people are here to see that author?" Mary Elizabeth asked a very good question after we stepped inside.

"Wait over there and I'll go find out what's going on." I gestured to the children's section where there looked to be enough room to squeeze in two more people.

I weaved in and out of the crowd. Fifi wiggled in my arms. She wasn't used to packed crowds like this when we went into buildings. I held her tighter. She'd get trampled if I let her down.

Abby and the rest of The Laundry Club ladies were nowhere to be found.

"Hey there, Mae." Trudy from the diner tugged on my jacket. "I guess the word is out around town that we have a celebrity staying here."

Standing right next to her was the woman writer I'd met at the diner.

"I wonder who told," I said, sarcastically giving each of them the stink eye. There'd been a long table set up in the open part of the library with just enough chairs for the members of The Laundry Club. There was another table covered with all of Abby's Tupperware products, which was odd.

"It was just too good to keep to myself." Trudy really thought it was okay to spill her guts. "I mean, it was already all over town and the diner about the scuffle with that photographer. It wasn't like I got on the telephone and went through the directory calling up everyone."

She called up enough people for this.

Out of the corner of my eye, I saw Abby scurry into the library office with Betts and Queenie following behind.

"Excuse me." Fifi and I pushed out of the crowd and into the office. "What on earth is going on?" I set Fifi on the ground.

"Nadine White hates me," Abby cried out. "I didn't get that social media post off the internet fast enough and it went viral."

"I told her not to worry about it. Everything has a plan." Betts tried to use all her wisdom about plans and creation on her, but Abby wasn't buying it.

"I told her to set up her Tupperware stuff and sell it. That way she could tell Nadine White that she was having one of them holiday bazaar sales." Queenie nodded. "And she can make a little spending cash. Everyone out there bought something." She held up the sheet with all the orders on it.

"That explains the Tupperware table," I said. "I did notice that. Have you told Nadine about this?"

"Told her. She is in there right now talking to her agent." Abby pointed to the door in the office. "It's the closet."

I let out a long sigh and walked over to the closet, flinging open the door.

Nadine was sitting on a box of copy paper with her agent next to her... in the dark.

"You!" Nadine gasped. "You did this, didn't you?"

"No, Nadine. I did not." I opened the door wide. "Please come out of there. We can talk about this."

"You don't understand. She has a real fear talking in front of people." The agent had a very stiff upper lip.

"I'm Mae West." I put my hand out. "We've not been properly introduced."

"Valerie Young, Nadine's agent." The tall, lanky woman with greasy, dishwater brown hair shook my hand. Her face softened when she realized I wasn't an enemy. "What do you suggest we do?"

"First, let me say that I'm sorry this has happened. It's not every day or even every month that such a well known celebrity visits Normal." Even though I had never heard of Nadine before this book Abby had us read, I did hear Mary Elizabeth's saying in my head; "Mae, dear, live like a peacock; don't ruffle your feathers unless you're prepared to fight."

Fighting with Nadine was the very last thing I needed on my plate this winter.

"Can you just read one or two pages of your book? I will address the crowd and talk about how we all need to respect your privacy while visiting our town." I continued as she began to process my words and walk out of the closet. "After you read a few pages, they will leave and then it'll just be our book club like we initially intended."

"That sounds do-able." Valerie nodded to Nadine. "She's right. This is a small town and honey, word gets around fast."

"Don't you write about small towns? You should know this." Abby made a great point.

"No. I write the love scenes. I have a ghost writer." Nadine might as well have slapped Abby across the face as hard as she could because it looked like Abby had just been beaten up. Her body had gone limp, her eyes dulled, and her jaw dropped. "My heart is in doing a cookbook for lovers."

It was as sad as the day a sweet child found out the real truth about Santa Claus.

"Okay." I gulped and gave Betts a look to get Abby out of there as soon as possible. "Let's get this done."

There wasn't much time. The crowd's murmurs had gotten a lot louder, louder than the library was supposed to be, and it was well past two o'clock.

I gestured for Nadine and Valerie to follow me, leaving Fifi in the office. Abby wasn't having any part of Betts cuddling her. When we all emerged from the office and walked up front, a blanket of silence once again fell upon the library.

"Wow. Bring an author to town and the crowd will come," I tried to make a joke. "Seriously, I'd like to thank Nadine White on behalf of Normal for picking our small town that maybe she can use in her novel while she's writing here."

"Liar," Abby whispered behind me. "Cookbook for lovers," she muttered. "Ridiculous."

"I'd like to think that we as a community can let Ms. White to have her privacy and enjoy the amazing winter season Mother Nature has gifted our part of the world. I'm sure if you see Ms. White out and about, she'll be amazing as she is, but please keep in mind that during those times, she's creating in her mind."

"Unlikely." Abby's voice was getting louder as the disgust was getting deeper.

"With that, Ms. White is going to read a couple of pages out of her novel *Cozy Romance in Christmas*."

Nadine was right. She wasn't the best public speaker. Her voice cracked and trembled with each word. While she tried to keep it together, I pulled Abby back into the office to try to get her to keep it together.

"I can't believe it." Abby thrust a fist into the air.

"I know. She's a hot mess." I wanted Abby to know that I understood where she was coming from.

"Hot mess? She's not even that, she's a lukewarm mess." Abby curled her lips in. They quivered. "I thought she was a real person. Come to find out, she didn't even write the parts I love. I love the scenery, the small town. I felt as if she were in my mind and heart."

I watched Abby go from mad to sad. She was going through the stages of grief, as if she'd just lost a best friend.

"Librarians get lost in the books. We take them personally. She comes in here to a book club and tells us that she has a ghost writer who adds all the cozy to her scenes. I skip over the romance part." Abby went right back into the angry stage. "She's a scam. A disgrace to the writing community." She pulled her phone out of her pocket. "Hashtag Nadine White is a hashtag scam."

"Okay." I grabbed her phone. "You're not going to do that. You're mad and this vindictive person you're pretending to be is not you."

I clicked the back button on her phone to erase the social media message.

"We don't need any bad publicity." I handed her phone back to her. "So, she's not what you thought she was. Who is? Look at me. When I came to Normal, everyone judged me by what my ex-husband had done. People just couldn't believe we lived under the same roof and I had no idea what he was doing in front of my face."

"That's true." She snapped her fingers." Nadine is no different than your husband. She is scamming everyone who is buying her books and funding her lifestyle."

"I think several authors have ghost writers, it's just that the public has no idea." I ran my hand down her arm. "Are you going to be okay?"

"I'm fine. Let's just get the crowd out of here and get this book club thing over with." Abby headed out the door with a little more foot stomping than normal, but it was to be expected. Abby's image of her idol had really been shattered.

I'd heard about this before, how social media paints authors as super nice and kind, but when you meet them in person, they aren't what they appeared to be. Hiding behind a screen on social media didn't appear to be any different than hiding behind the computer to write their books. In any case, all I cared about was Abby.

One thing Mary Elizabeth had always been good at was dispersing a crowd. When she was finished at an event she'd hosted, she got them out right quick and right now it was nice to have her and her skills.

"Who on earth has ever heard of selling Tupperware at a book club event?" Nadine snickered under her breath to Valerie.

"Excuse me!" Abby's hands formed fists. "I'm sorry that I ever thought you were a decent and sincere person. I honestly thought you understood small town life. Your heroine sells Tupperware in your series! Maybe that's why I decided to sell it myself!" Abby shook a finger at Nadine. "You. . ." she caught her breath. "You. . . you are disgrace to this library! Get out!"

Nadine's jaw dropped for a few seconds. Her face reddened, and she closed her mouth. Her eyes narrowed, and her jaw tensed.

"I've had enough of this for one day." She turned to Valerie. "I want to go back to the camper and get my things. Get me on the first flight out of here tonight."

"I'm not sure if the airport is even open since a blizzard is coming through." Valerie gestured out the window.

Without us even realizing it, the snow had fallen a lot faster and everything looked like it was covered by a fluffy blanket of white.

"Get me out of here!" Nadine yelled at the top of her lungs.

Abby ran off in a fit of sobs. Mary Elizabeth stood there with Betts, Queenie, and Dottie.

"I can take you back to the campground." The young woman who'd I'd talked to at the diner earlier said, shrugging her shoulders. "I've got a truck that'll drive through just about anything."

"Great." Nadine headed towards the door and then turned around. "Valerie, are you coming?"

"Yes. One second." She lifted her finger. "I'm sorry about this," Valerie apologized to me. "I thought everyone knew that because Nadine is so popular now that she simply can't do all of the writing with her schedule of appearances. We have several different writers who write various parts of the story, but the romance is really her thing."

Why was she telling me this? I didn't care.

"I guess what I'm saying is that Nadine is really a great woman and I think all of this has caught her off guard. She didn't bring any clothes to be seen in and the paparazzi showing up didn't help matters. She wants to get back to writing the entire book without having to rely on a ghost writer, so, please, give her some grace." She shrugged and looked at each of us. "It's all we ask while we are here."

"We're sorry it didn't go as planned. When Abby settles down, I'm sure she'll understand." I really didn't know where Abby's head was at the moment, but I knew she was very disappointed.

After Valerie left the bookstore and hopped into the woman's truck next to Nadine, there was a few moments of silence before Queenie started to laugh and bounce on her toes.

"We need a little oxygen in our muscles after that," Queenie huffed and transitioned her little dance into a Jazzercise grapevine. "By the looks of things, I'm going to be a little late for teaching my class."

"Yeah. It looks like a lot of things might be late or cancelled." I knew I wasn't being a good friend to Abby when all I could think about was my supper date with Hank and where it stood with this snow.

Queenie and I found Abby in the romance section, right in front of Nadine White's shelf that Abby had dolled up for the big occasion. She had made sure Nadine's books were displayed to perfection. The top of the bookcase had Nadine's framed bio photo alongside her framed bio. Abby had even gone as far as to list all of Nadine's achievements.

"All of those are lies." Abby pointed to the list of book awards. "She didn't deserve them. Whoever her ghost writer is deserves them." The anger in her voice was so strong and deep, I wasn't sure she was ever going to recover.

"Abby, why don't you come with me to release some of that steam?" Queenie jabbed the air as a growl expelled from deep within her gut as she twisted her core with each hit, jutting towards Nadine's framed photo.

CHAPTER SEVEN

Luckily, Betts had brought her big cleaning van. We all piled on top of the sweepers, spray bottles, and mops, making the most of our trip. The radio weather update confirmed that the Bluegrass Airport had shut down due to low visibility and ice on the runway. That part of the state must've been getting more wet snow, unlike the fluffy stuff we were getting.

Betts dropped Abby and Queenie off first, making the campground the last stop since it was further out of town. Queenie continued to badger Abby about going to Jazzercise. She was too mad to do anything, but Queenie was right. It would probably do Abby some good to let out some of that anger and steam before she popped like a pressure cooker.

Reluctantly, Abby got out of the car with Queenie after we talked her into getting out some of that aggression. This gave Dottie, Betts, and I some time to talk about Abby and how we were going to try to help her disgust this huge blow.

"What are we going to do about Abby? She's heartbroken." Betts gripped the wheel and drove the van very slowly along the curvy road leading back to Happy Trails.

"I hate how her idol shattered her." Dottie sighed.

"I know. I tried talking to her, but she wasn't very receptive. She wants to burn all of Nadine's books. I've never seen her so angry." I shook my head. "I would hate for Nadine to have this awful experience and then tell the world about it, undoing all the work Abby has done along with the rest of the town to get the economy back on track."

"True. It only takes one false claim and one stray tweet to put a whole world against you." Betts made an excellent point. "Even before you can prove the accusations aren't true."

"Mmmhhh." Dottie looked back at Mary Elizabeth. "What do you have to say? What if Abby was your daughter?"

"I would ask Abby what is it that she gets from books. Is it an escape? Because we know the books Nadine writes with all that happy ju-ju aren't reality. Abby needs to take stock in why she loves being a librarian and realize everything she sees with her own eyes isn't reality." She slid her eyes towards me.

My intuition told me she was not only trying to give that advice to Abby, but to me as well.

"That's an excellent point." Betts looked at me through her rear-view mirror. "I think I'll call her when I get home. I know Lester will want to take food to some of the older congregation members since the weather won't allow them to get out. Maybe I'll swing by her house and check on her."

"Remember, she's the youngest of us. She's not lived long enough to get too many disappointments, and this was a doozy." Dottie held on to the door handle when the tail end of the van fishtailed as Betts turned into the campground.

Valerie Young was standing by the door of the office, shivering, when we pulled up.

"Let me off at the office," I told Betts. "I can walk to my camper."

Betts stopped and before I got out, I unzipped my coat, putting Fifi inside and zipping it back up so just her head was sticking out. The things I did for her even shocked me. Who on earth was I turning into? I wondered and thanked Betts for the ride.

"Let me know how Abby is doing." I waved goodbye to them. "Hi, Valerie. Let's go inside and get out of the cold."

With my free hand, I dug into my purse to find the flamingo keychain that had the office and camper keys on it.

Henry was in the gator cart with the snow plow shoveling the road around the campground and clear the concrete pads of the campers. We didn't need anyone suing us. He was really good at his job.

"Can I make a pot of coffee?" I asked her and pulled my phone out of my bag. There weren't any missed calls or text messages.

Fifi had run over to her bed and curled up in a tight ball. I had enough time to brew some coffee, have a quick cup with Valerie, and get back to my place before I had to get ready for my visit with Hank, since he'd yet to cancel. There was no way I was canceling.

"I want to apologize again for Nadine's behavior today." Valerie stood next to me and watched me scoop the coffee grounds.

"You don't need to apologize for her. I think she's a big girl." I flipped on the coffeepot switch to brew.

"That's where you're wrong. She used to be very sincere and kind. She had this amazing vision of how she wanted to treat her readers and fans. She was so young when I took her on for representation." Valerie smiled at the memory. "In fact," she laughed, "I turned her down several times. She wasn't ready. She'd not experienced love and her love scenes were rather. . ." She flip-flopped her hand in the air, "rather. . .umm. . .G-rated."

"Well, she's caught up." I grabbed a couple of mugs and poured just enough before the entire pot brewed. "Creamer? Sugar?" I asked.

"Both." Valerie sat down in the chair and crossed her legs, swinging the top one. "I told her she needed to make herself a little softer while we are here."

"I thought you were going to get the first flight out of here." I took her the cup and the items to doctor it up.

"She was being. . .Nadine." She poured in more sugar than coffee, slowly stirring the cream in. "She has a tendency to go off at the hip and it's my job to clean up the aftermath."

"You're staying then?" I asked, to be sure I didn't need to send in Henry to clean the camper.

"As of now, we are staying. She needs the time to explore Normal and how everyday people live. She's forgotten that after all of her success. But she truly wants to get back to writing all the books herself." Valerie took a couple of sips of the coffee. "Did you know that Laura has written a book?"

"Laura?" I asked and sat down at my desk to face her.

"The young woman in your book club." Valerie gave me a strange look. It took me a second to realize she was talking about the young woman who took them home.

"She's not in our club. I just met her at the diner this morning. It was very nice of her to bring y'all out here from the library." Laura, I repeated in my head, so I could make it a point to thank her when I see her next.

"It was nice and those are the people Nadine needs to rub elbows with. In fact, I suggested Nadine take a look at Laura's manuscript. You know, give her a few pointers." Valerie wrinkled her nose. "We can get a write up in the paper how Nadine is living here for a few months, helping a local aspiring writer bring her dreams to life."

"Wow. That's nice of Nadine." I didn't see that coming.

"Oh, it was my idea. You know. . ." She rolled her eyes, "the cleaning up after the mess she's made. I don't want all the people in Normal to think Nadine White is a monster. Then we'll never sell another book or the new series."

"New series?" That was a little tidbit I could tell Abby to make her feel better.

"Like I said, Nadine wants to get back to the style she wrote when I first took her on as a client. More of the G-rated things you see on those mushy television channels. Books-made-for-TV types of things." She added more cream to her coffee and slowly stirred it. "This new series is unlike any of her past ones, so we are hoping a big publisher is going to pick it up. We have high expectations. After all, she is Nadine White."

"Yes. Yes, she is." I smiled, wondering exactly what it was Valerie had come to see me about. I looked at my phone. I'd been here long enough. "What was it you wanted to see me about?"

"I wanted to know if you could give me the address of that wonderful librarian. Nadine feels awful about what happened, and we'd like to pay her a visit. A peace offering of sorts." Valerie smiled.

She sure was good at her job of sweeping up after Nadine's mess.

"Like what?" I asked.

"We'd like to drop off a big basket of signed books for the library as well as have her take us around Normal tonight. Get to know the town. The small life. You know, make things right so she realizes Nadine was having an off day."

"Off day." I lifted my chin. "Is that what you're going to call it?"

"It is what we call it." Valerie's voice didn't quiver. It was strong and steady. She meant business. "The publisher is going to fly into the Bluegrass Airport in a couple of days to meet with her about the concept of her next book. I have to have her in the right mental state for that meeting. Everyone bends over backwards for her and she just doesn't see it."

"I'm sure Abby will be thrilled." I scribbled Abby's name and address on a sticky note, handing it to Valerie. All that other stuff she was telling me about publishers and concept just went right over my head. "Now, if you'll excuse me. I've got to be somewhere." I plucked a business card for the campground out of the small acrylic holder sitting on top of my desk and gave her it. "If you need anything through the night, our handyman, Henry, is on site and available twenty-four seven."

It was a nice little extra that made the tourists feel a little safer. It was interesting how they loved to hike the woods in the daylight, but the woods scared the bejeevers out of them at night.

"Thank you." She took the business card and put it on the sticky side of the note, folding them together and placing it in her pocket. "Please don't tell Abby about our plan. We like to surprise Nadine's fans."

"No problem. My lips. . ." I drew an invisible zipper across my lips and dusted off my hands.

CHAPTER EIGHT

There was a sense of relief that all had been worked out between Nadine and Abby because if it wasn't, it was going to be a long and cold winter. I didn't mean that to be about the weather either.

Poor Fifi was shivering as we headed back to the camper. I decided to take the long way around the lake to make sure all was well with the campground before I left for my big date. The last thing I wanted was a call from Dottie saying I had to come home from my date early due to someone at the campground needing something.

"I'm telling you, it's not going to sell!" Valerie's voice carried through the thin walls of the camper she and Nadine had rented. "No one is interested in that. Your readers want the fire. The sex. The romance. Don't you get it?"

There were some mumbles from another voice that could only be Nadine responding to an angry Valerie.

I held Fifi closer to my body, so she'd stay warm and not squirm or yelp. Call me nosy. I liked to think I was curious.

"This is ridiculous. If you think that I'm going to sign off on any sort of thing like that, then you're out of your mind! No one wants romance in the kitchen! The bedroom is where you write the words! That's what makes it steamy. Not a cup of pasta!" There was a pause before Valerie started yelling again. "Just like this camper! What on earth is going around in that head of yours to make you want to stay in this hick town for months? These very cold months? That's it! The cold has made you crazy!"

There was some stomping around, but I didn't know who it was. When I heard the footsteps coming closer to the door, I took off. I didn't want them to see me.

"Okay, sweet girl." I grabbed one of Fifi's sweaters from her drawer in my dresser.

It was the time of year she had to wear a little sweater all day and night. Tammy, her previous owner, did give me a slew of sweaters to pick from. After Fifi had babies from Rosco the pug, Tammy was all too happy to give me all of Fifi's wardrobe, which at this time in my life was larger than mine.

"You've got it made, little girl," I said to Fifi as I pushed around the hangers in the camper's small closet. "What about this one?" I pulled out a black sweater that was more form- fitting than the sweatshirts Hank was used to seeing me wear.

I held it up to my body and turned around. Fifi was doing a little tail jig on the bed, causing her whole body to shake with delight. I swear fashion was ingrained in the little white fur ball. Tammy was like Mary Elizabeth, ingraining it in Fifi by putting her in all the clothes, classes, and makeup in an effort to make her the best show dog around.

See where we both ended up. . .Happy Trails Campground.

"I think you're right." I twisted around the other way in the very small bedroom situated at the back of the camper and looked at my reflection in the full-length mirror I had attached to the wall.

Space was limited in campers. Well, my space was limited. We had many tourists that'd come in those big fancy campers and RVs that were truly like houses on wheels. I'd never realized just how many people actually lived their life full time as campers, going from state to state and exploring the US. It was truly awesome.

"With the only pair of skinny jeans I've got and those beautiful snow boots," I said with a hint of sarcasm, "this just might be the right outfit."

I held the hanger up against me with one hand and grabbed a wad of hair with my other. I pulled it up a bit, thinking I'd wear the messy curls up, and moved side to side to see what I'd look like from different angles.

Fifi yipped from the edge of the bed.

"You're right again." I let go of the moppy mess and let the curls fly out on all sides. "Down. There's no sense in trying to fix this mess with . . ." I glanced over the bed and looked on the night stand at the glowing clock. "Only five minutes!"

I threw the shirt down on the bed and quickly ran to the bathroom to grab a spit bath since it was all I had time for. The night had gotten away from me and I thought I had a little longer than five minutes to get ready.

Before I knew it, the five minutes were up and Hank was right on time. Fifi had warned me before I heard the knock at the door. She was jumping up and down near the front door of the camper. It was her way of telling me someone had pulled up.

I had barely enough time to swipe on some red lipstick to give my pale face a pop of color before the knock came. I took one last look at my face. One thing I did miss about having the lifestyle I had before was the monthly dermatologist appointments that kept my face in shape with peels. I had had terrible acne as a teen. Though Mary Elizabeth got me at an early age, she'd always complained that I should've gone to see a dermatologist for my skin way before she had fostered me. It was another dig I felt she'd made about my deceased parents. Maybe that was another reason I'd not liked living under Mary Elizabeth's roof. I felt she was always trying to put my parents down.

The louder the knock, the louder Fifi barked.

"Just go on in. Honey, if she's expecting you, then she knows you're here." Mary Elizabeth's voice travelled through the camper. When I came around the corner of the bathroom, she and Hank were standing in the combination family room and kitchen area of the camper chatting away like two old pals. "See, there's my baby girl. And look at her. She's beautiful just like they taught her in those fashion classes I stuck her in when she was fifteen." Mary Elizabeth's face beamed with pride.

"Hi." I looked directly at Hank and nearly wanted to die right there. "Can I see you for a minute in my bedroom?" I gave Mary Elizabeth the death stare.

"I'm sure she wants my opinion on her outfit." She fluttered her eyes at Hank, gently touching his arm as she walked past him. "Mmmmmm. . ." she hummed under her breath as she approached me. "I could sop him up with a biscuit," she growled, lifting her perfectly tweezed brows.

"What are you doing here?" I asked, sliding the accordion door to the bedroom shut, giving us what little privacy a camper had.

"I saw your light on and was coming by to drop off a little pecan pie I made today. I noticed you're a little too skinny." She elbowed me in the ribs. "And if you want to keep that hunk out there, it appears I arrived just in time."

"Listen, I'm so glad that you and Bobby Ray are having a wonderful time over there. Let's get one thing clear." I sucked in a deep breath and looked her square in her eyes. I wanted so bad to tell her that it was Bobby Ray who had invited her and make it known I had nothing to do with it.

Then she smiled. Her cheeks puffed out, and she smiled bigger. There was a touch of age in her eyes that I'd never seen before. The big old softie I'd become from all the warm welcomes the citizens of Normal had shown me over the past six months started to melt the hardness of my heart towards Mary Elizabeth.

Instead of giving her a piece of my mind and telling her I didn't want her around for Christmas, I swallowed that big breath and decided for my peace of mind that it was time to bury the hatchet. After all, it wasn't like she was moving to Normal. Her visit would be over soon.

"This is my first date with Hank." I bit back the anger. "Do you think I look okay?"

Mary Elizabeth clapped her hands in delight before she rubbed them across my shoulders like she was getting off some lint. Her mouth opened, and I waited to take the blow about how I needed to do something different or how my hair was unruly. She closed her mouth and smiled.

"You look beautiful." Her words were simple and sincere. "You are the most perfect you there ever was. You've truly grown up to be an amazing individual. Though I didn't raise you, I do hope that I had some hand in how you've turned out."

My eyes watered. This was the first time I'd ever heard words come out of her mouth that I felt were honest as the humility covered her face.

"I know I wasn't a perfect foster mom," her voice cracked, and she lifted her hands around her neck. The strand of pearls cascaded down the front of her as she held one end of the strand pinched between her fingers. "I hope we can sit down while I'm here and make amends."

She reached up and over my head, placing the pearls around my neck and clipping the clasp together. Then she adjusted the necklace, placing it perfectly around my neckline.

"I do love you and Bobby Ray as if I had birthed you." She turned me around to face the full length mirror, her hands on each of my arms, her eyes staring at me over my shoulder. "Perfect touch."

I gulped back the lump in my throat. I lifted my hands to Mary Elizabeth's precious pearls that I'd once gotten grounded for after she caught me trying them on when she was in the shower so many years ago and ran my fingers along them.

"Are you sure I can wear them?" I asked when I realized they did make the outfit truly amazing.

"Wear them?" Her hands squeezed my arms. "They are yours now."

There was no denying the tone of her voice. She meant it. The stern and final squeeze of her hands told me so.

"Now, before we forget and get lost in this crazy moment, you get out there to that man waiting for you." Mary Elizabeth always did know how to diffuse a situation when she knew it was getting too heavy. "I'd love to keep my foster grand-dog."

"You're kidding, right?" I gave her the side eye.

"No. I'd love to. Just show me where the remote control is because I love that Real Housewives show and it's about to come on." She did not just say that.

"Who are you and where did you put Mary Elizabeth?" I asked in a joking way.

"You only know the mother side of me, which was what I had to be when you kids were growing up. Now you get the fun side of Mary Elizabeth," she referred to herself in third person, ripping open the accordion door before she trotted out of the bedroom in her white furry snow boots.

"That was interesting." Hank walked around the side of his truck and opened the passenger door for me.

"What? Hank Sharp opening the door for me? Or the fact my foster mom has showed up and decided to be someone I don't recognize?" I asked. "I'm sorry," I immediately apologized before I hoisted myself up into the truck.

Hank leaned up against that open door, his body shielding me from the chilly winter breeze.

"Sorry for what?" His big grin reached his green eyes, lifting them at the corners. "I finally get to know the real May-bell-ine. When you asked her how you look? You look amazing." He winked, slamming the passenger door. My heart did all sorts of flip flops in ways it's never flopped before.

"I guess you heard us in the other room?" I wiggled around nervously in the seat and adjusted the heat vents on my side.

"It's not like we weren't ten feet from each other with a tiny door separating us." He had both hands on the wheel, slowing taking the road through Happy Trails. "I think it's interesting to meet the woman who fostered you after your parents' deaths. I mean, I'm sure it's hard to take in a teenager."

"You know all about that?" When I looked over at him, we were passing Dottie Swaggert's camper. She had the curtain pulled back and waved at me with a big grin on her face.

"When someone by the name of Mae West decided to blow into

Normal, Kentucky, with the attitude you had, I had to know what this gal was all about." He leaned over the wheel, looking past me and then the other way before he pulled out to the main road leading into Normal. "Of course I looked you up, even though I knew about your past with your ex. Then I really got to know you after you decided to put your nose into my investigations."

"Listen, I think I have a knack for that sleuthing stuff." I teased as he belted a big belly laugh. "But you don't have to worry about that anymore."

"Is that right?" His southern drawl gave me goose bumps all over my body.

"I'm sure there's not going to be any more murders of people I know. Three is plenty. If we could just skip the rest of this month and get to the new year, I'd be all for it." I looked out the window at the snow. "It sure is coming down out there. I didn't know you had a truck."

"Yeah. I think everyone in this part of Kentucky has one since we have the national park and curvy roads." He continued through town and past the library, which was the last building on the street.

"Maybe I should get a truck," I made mention.

"I'll be more than happy to take you anywhere you want to go." He reached over and touched my hands I had folded in my lap. "I'm sorry. Was that too forward?"

"No. Not at all." I liked how his hand was heavy on top of mine. For some odd reason, it made me feel safe and gooey inside. I liked that. "It looks like Nadine is going to see Abby."

Nadine White was walking up the steps of the library holding a big basket.

"Her agent told me they were going to drop off a big basket of goodies and books for Abby at the library as a way of not only apologizing but to make peace."

"I heard about that whole scuffle thing when I called to check on Ms. White before I picked you up. She seemed awfully concerned with that photographer this afternoon and I just told her that I couldn't be hired on the side since I was going to be on forest ranger duty a few times during her visit." He took the next road on the left. There weren't any street lights, but the moon shined so bright off the snow there was barely any need for the truck's headlights to show us the way.

"I wished the internet at The Laundry Club hadn't gone out just as Abby put it on social media that Nadine White was going to be in town." I could feel my shoulders start to relax a little more and I let my fingers entwine with his. I felt like a teenager going on a date.

"Abby is the one who let the world know Nadine was here?" He shook his head.

He turned the truck into a parking lot where there were a lot of other cars parked in front of a big red barn. The Red Barn was the name posted across the top of the barn near the open door to what was a hay loft at one time.

"I've never been here. I've heard about this place and they do have some flyers at the campground office for tourists, but I've never checked it out." The snow on top of the barn roof sparkled in the moonlight. The mountains of the Daniel Boone National Park shadowed in the background made the entire scene as pretty as a picture.

"I'm honored to be the first to bring you." Hank put the truck in park. "Now, you wait right there because I'm going to be the southern gentleman you don't think I can be and open your door."

"I never. . ." I started to protest his observation of me. And started back up when he opened the door, "To clarify, I never thought you weren't a southern gentleman." I got out of the truck. "I said that you were a different type."

"You told me that Ty was sincere and thoughtful. True to his southern roots." Hank had a good memory.

"But you didn't hear me say that I thought you were the protective type of southern gentleman." Which was the truth.

When I first opened up my heart to even think about a relationship, I was charmed by Ty's sweet demeanor and attention, which was what I needed at that moment in time. It was Hank's protectiveness and making sure I had everything I needed in the long term that really stole my heart.

"You are a listener. When I mentioned that I needed to plow the campground's gator for snow removal, you found me one." I was about to give another example, but Hank had a different idea.

He put his finger on my lips. His large hand took my face and held it gently, forcing me to look at him. There was a deep softness to his green eyes that I'd never seen before.

"You will always be safe with me. I will always protect you." He leaned in and his lips touched my lips like a soft whisper.

He pulled back, leaving me standing there with my lips puckered and ready for more. When I opened my eyes, he was grinning.

"I had to get that out of the way or it would have been on my mind all night." He reached down and grabbed my hand, leaving me breathless and speechless. "Looks like I did it again. I left Mae West speechless for the second time in six months."

"Stop it." I teasingly smacked his arm and let him lead me into the barn.

If you'd told me that an old farm barn could be romantic, I would have laughed and told you about some really neat place in New York City that'd charm the pants right off you when you stepped inside, but this old barn was so charming. I had not been to a nice restaurant and almost a year now, so maybe that's the reason I immediately fell in love with the place.

Long gone were the old stalls , hay lofts, and dirt floor. The inside was completely open with exposed wood beams. I wasn't sure if they were original to the barn, but if they weren't, someone had gone to great lengths to make it look like they were. Each wood beam had strands of small and round light bulbs that were turned down just enough so you could see what you were eating but felt as if you were under the moon.

Tables draped with white linen tablecloths were scattered around with a romantic red candle in a lantern in the middle of each. Some of the tables had two chairs while others had four.

Along the back of the barn was a long bar with floor to ceiling shelves of any Kentucky bourbon and wine you could imagine. There was no mistaking the pride the Red Barn took in their spirits.

To the right of the bar, there was just enough space for a band. Tonight the band was playing some jazz, which I loved.

"Reservation for Sharp." Hank held my hand so tight as he proudly said his name.

"Please follow me." The hostess grabbed two menus and walked ahead of us. "Can I start you off with some wine?"

Hank rattled off something that I wasn't familiar with. Really, I wasn't familiar with much alcohol other than a beer every now and again.

"What do you think?" He asked a very good question that I wasn't sure how to answer.

"What do I think?" I needed clarification. Was he asking about the kiss or the restaurant?

Both were amazing.

"About the atmosphere?" He suddenly looked very amused. "Wait. You were thinking I was asking about me kissing you."

"No, I wasn't." I tried to play it off.

"Oh, Mae West. Yes, you were." He gave me a friendly smile, bantering back and forth with me in a relaxed manner. "I'm getting so good at reading you now. I was a little off when you first moved here, but you aren't as transparent as you want to be."

"I don't know what you're talking about." I tossed some curls behind my shoulder. Had I really lost the touch of not showing all my cards, I wondered.

He laughed triumphantly.

"Stop it." I folded my arms in front of me. "Stop making fun of me."

"I'm not. You're cute." Those two words sounded so odd coming from him.

Cute and the six-foot, dark haired, green eyed and just enough muscles under his shirt to make him hunky didn't seem to go together, but he pulled it off.

"Cute?" My jaw dropped.

"Gorgeous and I'd like to revisit that kiss later. I just knew I couldn't sit across from you like this if it were still burning in my head what it would be like to kiss you. And I'm glad to say it didn't disappoint."

The waitress had come over with the bottle of wine Hank had mentioned to the hostess and did the whole swirl test. It was something my ex would do at the restaurants we visited in the city before the scam he pulled over everyone's eyes imploded and blew up my life.

Hank gave her the nod and she poured two glasses of the pinot he'd picked out.

"To a real first date of many." Hank lifted his glass in the air, starting off the first toast of many to come in our future.

Both of us had gotten the steak special. The conversation flowed with ease like we'd known each other for a longer period of time. I got to know about his family and how they still lived in Normal. He'd even slipped and said that he couldn't wait for me to meet them, which made me believe this was more than a onetime gig. The way things were going, that sounded good to me. I knew I wasn't ready to make a big commitment, but spending time with Hank was a responsible way for me to have companionship and take baby steps in that direction.

"My mom loves Ginger." He lit up when he talked about one of Fifi's puppies that he'd given to his mother as a gift. "Ginger goes everywhere with her."

"I love that. What does her fur look like?" I questioned if the mix of poodle and pug did any sort of damage to the little ones. Since I had given the other puppies to tourists after I'd made them fill out adoption paperwork with the local SPCA and undergo a background check, I'd not kept in touch with them.

"She looks like a poodle, but she has tan fur, not white. What amazed my mom the most was that she could walk into any gun shop and walk out with a gun in fifteen minutes while it took five weeks to adopt a dog." He shook his head. "As someone who carries as an officer of the law, I agree with my mom."

"I'm so glad the ASPCA has that process because I was so worried about the safety of Fifi's babies." I wanted to keep them all, but there was no way I could have them in a camper. Fifi was already high maintenance, and I couldn't imagine having several more like her.

When the band played, we both sat back with our wine and listened with ease, never once trying to make conversation or force it along. It was nice to be able to go out and enjoy another adult. Especially a good looking one that did have good kissing skills, though I wouldn't admit that at this point.

"I hate to see the night end." Hank hinted around to extending it once we got back to the camper.

"That's strange," I noted when we drove past the library. "Abby is still there and it's after ten."

Nothing in Normal was open past eight or nine p.m. Most businesses closed around six p.m. and the library was one of them.

"That is odd." Hank pulled the truck over to the curb right behind the rental I'd seen barreling out of the campground that Nadine White had been driving.

"Oh, maybe she and Nadine have bonded. I'm sure they're gabbing over books." I shrugged Hank's concern off.

"I'd rather go check it out. That Nadine sure was upset about people finding out she was here." He threw the gear shift into park. "You wait right here."

As if.

I jumped out of the truck as soon as I saw him walk around the front of it.

"Really?" His brow lifted with amused contempt.

"She's my friend. I want to make sure she's OK." Not that I thought anything was wrong, but I did kinda wanted Nadine to see that I was with Hank because I seen the look on her face at the Normal Diner this morning when she was sitting across from him.

Hank left the southern gentleman from earlier at the restaurant behind as he bolted up the front steps of the library. It was a very old Victorian house that'd been converted into the town's library. There were concrete steps leading up to a wraparound porch where Abby had placed rockers for readers' enjoyment. She even left them out in the winter along with a basket next to each one with a quilt made by women in the Women's Club of Normal.

Hank opened the front door.

"That's weird too." I bit on my lip as a tiny bit of worry settled into my gut. "I've been here before when she's putting newly cataloged books on the shelf after hours and she always locks the door."

The loudest scream I've ever heard came from the office.

I stood there in slow motion as I watched Hank draw the gun from the hidden holster under his shirt. I shoved past him, running towards the office. It was as though my feet had a mind of their own.

"Abby?" I questioned when I got to the door and noticed she was standing over Nadine White on the floor. "Did you scream?"

I could feel Hank behind me.

"Abby?" Hank called.

She stood with her back to us. My eyes drew down her body until they saw the bloody knife dangling from her fingers.

She turned around. Her eyes hollow.

"She's dead," she replied in a small frightened voice.

CHAPTER NINE

"Let me have the knife," Hank talked gingerly to Abby.
She looked down at her hand as though she didn't realize she was holding a knife. She blinked a few times, like she was trying to bring herself back to reality. Like a robot, she lifted her hand in the air.

Hank grabbed the handkerchief out of his pocket and took the knife. As I watched, I knew he was doing his detective thing by taking the knife so as not to disturb the fingerprints. After I'd helped him a few other cases over the past six months, I'd watched more crime television than one woman should in a lifetime.

"Why don't you just come out here and sit." Hank guided her out of the office and completely ignored me like I wasn't even there.

Nadine White's eyes were open. Her clothes were tidy and neat, but the blood was still gushing from the side of her neck where there appeared to be a stab wound to her carotid artery. I bent down next to her, careful to barely breathe and not touch a thing, to see if there were any signs of life. Her chest was still. I put my hand over top her mouth and nose and there was nothing coming out.

"What are you doing! Get back!" Hank had turned into the Hank I didn't like.

"I was just seeing if she was alive," I tried to explain myself, pushing off my knees to stand.

"Listen, I know you're trying to help here, but I've called backup and the best thing you can do is go out there and talk to Abby. Find out what the heck happened here." He ran his large hand through his hair before he bent down and used his hands to feel for a pulse.

There was an icy twist around my heart with the sudden realization that Hank thought Abby had done this.

"Wait, you don't think Abby had anything to do with this?" I asked him like he was out of his mind.

"Do you see anyone else?" He asked me sarcastically. "She had the knife. She was stunned."

"She's in shock," I reminded him as I left the room before I took the knife and did a number on him myself.

Abby was sitting in the swivel chair at the reference desk where she sat most days to welcome library patrons. Her face was pasty white. Her eyes stared blankly in front of her. Her hands were shaking.

"Abby," I whispered her name to let her know I was coming up behind her. "Abby."

When I touched her she flinched, jerking around with her hands fisted in front of her.

"It's okay." There wasn't life in her eyes. "It's me, Mae," I reminded her who I was because she didn't look at me. She looked through me, so I wasn't sure if she was seeing me even though I was the only one standing right there.

With the same look on her face, she put her shaky hands back down in her lap. Her chest lifted up and down.

"Abby." I squatted down next to her. "Do you know me?"

Slowly she nodded, her eyes slide over to look into mine. She blinked a few times, finally focusing on me. Her mouth gaped open. Her breath heaved in and out.

"Mae," she gasped in desperation. "Nadine is dead."

"Yes, honey." I ran a hand down her hair. "I know."

"She. . .she. . .," her voice trembled. Her head turned, eyes glazed over facing the library, away from me. "She was lying there."

"Lying there?" My inner voice alerted my brain to ask more questions, even in Abby's fragile state. "Abby, what do you mean by she was lying there."

"She was lying there. Her eyes open. The knife. . ." Her nostrils flared up and down, her chest heaved up and down as the sound of her breath went in and out of her nose. "Oh my God, Mae," she cried out, her eyes filled with tears. "Nadine is dead." She buried her head in her hands.

I stood back up and bent over her, wrapping my arms around her while she sobbed. A couple police officers rushed past us and filed into the office where Hank was.

"Abby. I'm going to need you to help me out here." I pulled away when I felt her breathing return to normal. "What happened between you and Nadine?"

"What do you mean?" She gulped for breath.

"Did you get into another argument?" I asked. "Did you fight?"

"What are you talking about?" Her brows furrowed. She was obviously in shock and not in her right mind.

"You do understand that Nadine White was found dead in your office with you standing over her with a knife," I looked her square in the eyes.

"Yes. I found her there." She nodded, searching my face.

"You found her in your office and you fought with her?" I asked, trying to get to what happened or jar her memory.

"She was dead. I pulled the knife out of her neck," she cried out, sobbing again.

"Wait." I bent back down and put my hand on her leg. "Are you telling me that you found her in your office already stabbed?"

"Yes." She nodded.

"This changes everything," I muttered.

"Do you think I stabbed her?" Abby looked at me like I had five heads. "Mae?"

"I've got to get you out of here." I glanced around to see who was near us. "Abby, I need you to focus more than ever on me." I held her face and made her look into my eyes. "Hank and I found you standing over Nadine's body, holding the knife. It looks like you killed her, and Hank is going to think that."

"I didn't." She jerked her head around, looking behind her. "Where is he? I'll tell him."

"You're going to have to get it together." I glanced over at the library's complimentary Keurig station. "You sit right here, and I'll grab us a cup of coffee."

"I don't want a coffee." Abby shrugged.

"I'm going to need you to drink a coffee to get you out of this fog. We. . . I need to know exactly what happened tonight." I didn't leave her any room for arguing with me. She didn't realize the severity of the situation and what it looked like for her.

The Keurig rumbled to life when I put the pod in the holder and pressed the largest option available.

"Keep an eye on her." I overheard one of the officers say to another one. "She's the killer. From what Hank said, he's not had a minute to ask her anything."

Killer? The word knotted in my gut. Abby couldn't kill anyone.

I doctored up my coffee with creamer and slowly stirred it in, more than usual, so I could hear more conversations between the two cops.

"Why'd she kill her? Do we know?" One of them asked.

"Fan turned psycho. I've seen it all now." The other's voice dripped with a hint of laughter.

I grabbed my cup and moseyed over to Abby just in case I heard anything else, but I didn't. The rest of officers were standing watching Colonel Holz push the church cart through the automatic front doors of the library.

Colonel Holz was the county coroner. I'd yet to meet him properly, but there was never a better time than right now, especially since I was going to have to figure out, with his help without a doubt, who really killed Nadine White.

"Hi, Dr. Holz." I walked next to the church cart. "I'm Mae West and

Nadine White had rented a camper in my campground. I sure hate that she's dead. What do you think I should tell the family?"

I pulled that question out of nowhere, a little proud of myself. There was a place on the rental form that asked for next of kin. Since we were a hiking and camping community, there were more than just hiking accidents, there were also critters to deal with, including dangerous ones. I liked to have the emergency contact or next of kin on the form, so we had a way of getting in touch with someone.

"Well, you're gonna have to take that up with Detective Sharp. I'm not sure what's going on until I take a look at the body. I suggest you let Detective Sharp call the family." The Colonel wasn't budging.

Abby's face flushed white again when she noticed the coroner. She started to sob all over again. It didn't go unnoticed that the two officers next to the Keurig station nudged each other.

"Abby." I rushed over to her with the coffee. I held it out to her. She waved it off. "Listen, I know you're in shock."

"Outta the way!" The boisterous voice pushed through the officers. When they parted, Queenie was leading The Laundry Club gals straight over to us. "What are you lookin' at, Violet Rhinehammer?" Queenie stopped and looked at a woman who'd come in right before them. "You better sweep your own back porch before sweeping somebody else's." Queenie pointed to the notebook Violet had in her hand. "You can quote me too."

After Queenie said that, I recognized Violet Rhinehammer as the new reporter for the local newspaper. There'd been some gossip down at The Laundry Club about her, but I reckoned it was all talk and Queenie just flapping her lips. I wished I'd listened a little more closely now.

From what I knew about reporters from the crime shows, they could be valuable with information and with ways on how they got that information.

"What in the blue blazes is going on here?" Dottie asked, assessing Abby.

Betts Hager had already rushed to Abby's side and was talking to her like a good pastor's wife. It was her natural ability to comfort and soothe. I wanted to get to the bottom of it.

"I can't get much out of Abby, but I found her standing over Nadine White's body holding a bloody knife." I heard the words come out of my mouth and knew it didn't sound good.

"We need to get her out of here." Queenie's brows lifted underneath her purple headband. "Or they'll arrest her on the spot."

"Where we going to take her?" Dottie asked.

"We can take her to my place," I suggested. "I don't have a car, so someone else is going to have to drive us."

Out of the corner of my eye, I noticed one of the officers next to the Keurig had walked into the library office.

"That's right." Dottie smacked the air with her hand. "How was the big date? I seen you two leaving Happy Trails."

"We can talk about that later." Betts had left Abby's side. "We need to get her out now."

Queenie already had Abby on her feet and Dottie had grabbed Abby's coat along with her purse. I helped Abby put her arm in the sleeve of her coat.

"My phone." She pointed to the phone next to the computer on the reference desk and Dottie grabbed it on our way out towards the door.

"Mae, where do you think you're taking her?" Hank's voice came from behind us. We all stopped and slowly turned around. "Abby, you can't leave. I need to question you."

"Question her?"

"Hank?" Violet walked over to us. I didn't like how she said his name with her sweet, small, accented tone. "I'd love to talk to you." She ran a fingernail down his arm with a little wink.

"Hold on, Violet." He looked back at me. "Abby needs to stay here right now."

Violet started to scribble away on that pad of hers. I wanted to grab it and rip it apart.

"Abby is in no state of mind to be here and unless you want to arrest her she's going home with me. You can come by there if you need to question her." I gave Violet a good hard stare. "You know exactly where I live since you picked me up for our date there earlier."

"Date?" Violet questioned with a dumbfounded look.

"Yeah, honey. Your nest isn't the only one he's been buzzing around." Queenie grabbed Abby by the elbow and walked her out of the library.

"Mae," Hank hurried to my side. My pace had quickened after I heard Queenie's words. "I need to question her." He pulled me to the side when we made it outside. "You and I both know what we saw."

"I'm not saying we didn't see her standing over the body with the knife." I wanted to be clear to what I saw. "But she didn't do it."

"Mae," he said with an exhausted sigh, running his hand through his hair. "You've got to be kidding me. It's cut and dry. Even you said earlier that Abby was devastated her idol was a fraud."

"I didn't say those exact words." I'd forgotten about me telling him about that and now I wished I'd just kept my big mouth shut.

"That's what you meant and you know it. I can't just forget what happened between them. Plus we saw Nadine walking into the library with that basket of stuff to make an apology, according to you." He had the memory of a steel trap.

"According to Valerie, her agent." I snapped my fingers. "By the way, where's she at? She might've set this whole thing up, making Abby look like the killer. Valerie and Nadine had an argument earlier at the campground."

Hank's chest expanded as he took a silent deep breath. I knew he knew I was right. There could be more than just one person not happy with Nadine.

"Listen, I'm going to let you take her out of here, but you have to go straight to the department before you take her to your place. I want her fingerprinted and her nails checked and to see if there are any marks of a struggle or anything on her body that has to do with Nadine White." He stopped talking when the doors slid open and Colonel was pushing the church cart back out of the library with a sheet covering Nadine's body.

Betts already had Dottie, Abby, and Queenie loaded up in her mini-van.

"Got it?" He asked.

"Fine." I over exaggerated the word to prove my point that I wasn't happy about it.

"And I'm sorry our date ended like this." He leaned in as though he was about to give me a goodnight kiss.

"Yeah, yeah." I took a few steps backwards, meeting his eyes and seeing his confusion. "See ya."

CHAPTER TEN

"Was Hank about to give you a kiss back there?" Betts asked me while Agnes Swift took Abby back to the room where they were going to fingerprint her and look her over really good to see if she'd had any markings on her.

"Let's just say that there was a lot of chemistry between us before he went and accused Abby of killing Nadine White." I huffed, crossing my arms across my chest while we waited in the police department.

"Mae, he's doing his job. This shouldn't have anything to do with what the two of you might feel for each other." Betts was always the voice of reason.

"Is there a history with Violet Rhinehammer?" I asked, taking the heat off the amazing date that Hank and I had before we decided to stop by the library.

"I think they dated a little on and off, maybe a few months were serious." Betts made it seem like it was no big deal. "Her mom is in our prison group. She talks about Violet on the bus rides over and she tells me how Violet is so wrapped up in making a career for herself that Violet has no time for a social life."

"Her career is being a reporter for the newspaper?" I laughed, thinking it wasn't much of a career aspiration.

"I think she sees it more as an opportunity to gain some experience with research and following crime leads. That's where they put her. In the crime and search and rescue division since we seem to have a lot of that around Normal lately." Betts folded her hands in her lap. "I'm just not sure what's happening around here lately."

"With growth, like the economy and the boom in the camping business, there's bound to be more crimes." It was just an observation I had made. "I'm telling you that I just don't think Abby killed Nadine White."

The door to the department flew open, Valerie Young on the other side. She ran over to the desk of the officer closest to her, demanding to talk to someone about Nadine White.

When she turned around and saw us, she didn't wait for the officer's answer. She darted towards us.

"Mae, where's Nadine? What's going on?" She asked, out of breath.

"Why don't you have a seat," I said and patted the chair next to me.

"I don't want to sit. I got a call from the paparazzi asking me about Nadine's murder. I went back to the camper and she wasn't there. The car wasn't there. The only thing I knew to do was to come here after Nadine didn't answer her phone." Valerie's eyes darted around the station.

"It's true. Nadine's body was found tonight." Betts took over the situation, which was probably for the best since she had some experience in dealing with deceased people's family members.

It was part of the pastor's wife thing she did.

"What?" Valerie fell into the chair. I watched her body language like the TV sleuths did. "Where's the hospital?"

"She's dead, Valerie." Betts was as matter of fact as you could get. "She's been murdered and that's why we are here."

Valerie fell to the floor. One of the officers hurried over and helped her to her feet while Betts and I tried to do the best we could.

"We'll take her back to get checked out by the doctor." The officer maneuvered Valerie's limp body out of the room and back down the hallway. The same hallway where they'd taken Abby.

"How much longer?" Dottie looked at her watch. "I've got to get my hair in my curlers before too long or they won't have enough time to set right before I have to be at work in the morning."

"Like we know how much time." Queenie stood up, pushing her arms over her head before she did a forward bend, planting her palms on the department floor. She curled back up and did a few body twists to each side before she walked over to the cork board. "Hey, y'all." She ripped a piece of paper from the thumb tack. "The Ice Capades are coming to town. We've got to go."

"Coming to Normal?" Dottie asked.

"Nope. Lexington. But we can all go." She walked over and handed the paper to Dottie. Dottie passed it down the line and back to Queenie who folded the paper in half and stuck it down in her bra. "I've been dying to see them. It's like a holiday tradition."

"I think we need to see what's going on with Abby before we make any plans." I stood up when Abby turned the corner with Agnes.

"Here you go." Agnes patted Abby. "I told you your friends were here," she said, her jaws sagged. She was the cutest eighty-year-old I'd ever seen. She had short gray hair and wore a pair of black polyester pants with a long-sleeved Normal Police Department shirt. "How did your date go?" She winked at me.

"Date." Abby's shoulders slumped. "Mae, I'm so sorry this ruined your date. Leave. Go finish your date."

"Honey, you're more important than a silly date." I left out the fact Hank was back at the crime scene and that's another reason we ended it. I knew she wasn't in her right mind to even put that together in her head. It was important that she knew she was supported, even if the odds were stacked against her.

I nodded for Agnes to have a private conference to the side while the other gals got Abby's coat back on her.

"Thank you for being so nice to her." I wanted to let Agnes know how much she was appreciated.

"She's in shock. She needs to go to sleep." Agnes glanced back at Abby over my shoulder. "I told Hank that the doctor didn't find nothing on her. I don't think she did it."

"Did she say anything to you about it?" I asked Agnes. She'd always been so forthcoming in the other investigations even though Hank hated it.

"Not a word came out of her mouth. The doctor asked her all sorts of questions. He said he'd give her a prescription to sleep, so if you need it, give me a call and I'll get it to you. But right now, if she gets some sleep, her memory might just come right back in the morning." Agnes gave a sympathetic smile. "Hank asked if you were here."

"Thanks, Agnes." I didn't want to get into all that. "I think it's best we get Abby back to my place."

There was dead silence in the minivan on the way home. The cleaning supplies in the back of Betts's minivan rattled as she drove the curvy road back to Happy Trails. The compacted snow groaned under the tires as the snow continued to fall in big flakes, faster than the windshield wipers could clear.

"I'm taking you to my house for the night." I ran my hand down Abby's hair and helped her out of the van once we got there.

"Do you need help?" Dottie asked.

"No. I'm just going to put her to bed. I'll call y'all in the morning. We've got a lot to discuss," I said before I shut the door behind us.

Fifi jumped and yipped for Abby to give her some affection. Abby smiled and spoke to Fifi. It was the first sign of life still left in her.

"I'm going to go lay down if you don't mind." Abby's voice was soft.

"I think that's a great idea." I agreed with her. "I'll take Fifi out to do her business and check on you when I come back in. You know where everything is so help yourself." I opened the refrigerator and took out a bottle of water. "Put this by the bedside in case you need a drink later."

She took the water and disappeared into the bedroom of my RV. Fifi danced around at the door waiting for me to open it. She darted down the steps. I followed her. A thick silence filled the space around me. An eerie feeling blanketed me.

I looked up in the sky for reassurance that all was well, but the big snowflakes hid a lot of the stars and moonlight that made me feel calm. I glanced across the lake at the camper Nadine and Valerie had rented.

The twinkling lights swayed from the night breeze. I wondered about Nadine's personal life.

Did she have any family or friends that were going to miss her over Christmas while she was here? Did she plan to go somewhere for Christmas? What on earth was her story.

"Hey, girl." Fifi brought me out of my thoughts as she bounced up in the air wanting me to pick her up. "Let's go for a little walk."

My keys were still in my pocket and taking a night stroll up to the office to get a look at Nadine's contract sounded like a pretty good idea. There was no way I was going to fall asleep. There was too much adrenaline pumping inside of me from all the questions I had about Nadine.

Dottie's camper was dark. I bet she smoked a cigarette, put her pink sponge curlers in her hair, and headed straight to bed. The warmth of the office felt good on my chilly cheeks when I opened the door. Fifi ran over to her little bed after I put her down.

The files on my desk were the packets from the renters staying in the campground right now. I kept them on my desk from the time they checked in until they checked out for easy access. I was glad I didn't have to go searching the storage unit where we kept all the files after they checked out. The office was too small for any sort of storage cabinets.

The office was plenty big enough for our needs. There were two desks – mine and Dottie's – with two chairs in front of each, where the renters sat to sign their rental agreements when they checked in. Oh, and there was a coffee station and Fifi's bed on the floor between our desks.

I sat down and opened Nadine's file with her rental agreement. There was one contact she'd put down for an emergency and it was someone by the name of Dawn Gentry. I quickly wrote the name and phone number down. I knew it was something Hank would want to know.

I picked up the phone and hesitated before I dialed Dawn's number. I was torn about whether to let Hank call her or to call her myself. Per the agreement, I had full permission to reach out to Dawn.

"Hello?" A very sleepy voice answered.

"Is Dawn Gentry there?" I asked.

"This better be good for you waking me up. I better've won a million dollars." She was as sassy as Nadine. No wonder they were friends like Nadine stated on the contract.

"I'm sorry, but do you know Nadine White?" I asked.

"You mean Nadine Dembrowski?" She asked. "Nadine White is her pen name."

"Oh." I looked at the name she'd registered under and she'd written White. "Yes, if that's her real name." I scribbled it down. "She's the author of *Cozy Romance in Christmas*."

"Yeah, what about her?" Dawn sounded a little more awake.

"I'm Mae West from Happy Trails Campground where Nadine White… Dembrowski," I corrected myself, "rented a camper from me for the winter."

"Is she in jail?" Dawn didn't sound amused.

"Jail? Um. . .No." Odd, I thought. "She listed you as her emergency contact and I'm sorry to tell you that Nadine has been murdered."

"What?" Dawn was fully awake. "Nadine Dembrowski? Are you sure? I mean, I knew it was a crazy idea when she told me she was going to stay in some camper in Kentucky while she tried to write some sort of cookbook, but I didn't think it was dead crazy."

"Unfortunately, it's true. Valerie Young is staying with her and she's going to identify the body for the local sheriff's department, but since Nadine had listed you as her emergency contact, I thought you might be able to get in touch with her family." I could feel the tension over the phone line as Dawn processed everything I was telling her.

"God, I knew she and Valerie were having that big contract dispute and I told her not to kill Valerie. I never figured it'd be the other way around." Her words nearly stopped my heart.

"Valerie?" I asked a bit stunned.

"Yeah. You did say Valerie Young, right?" she asked. I could hear some fidgeting on the other end of the phone. "What town are you in? What airport?"

"I did say Valerie Young. Normal, Kentucky. Bluegrass Airport." I rattled off the answers. "Back to Valerie, did you say they are arguing over a contract?"

"Yes. Nadine told me that she was going to sign a contract without an agent, which means she was letting Valerie go. You know, in the publishing world today, authors don't really need a middleman anymore. Nadine knew that. Now she wanted to write the books she's always wanted to write. Not use a ghost writer to help her."

I was so glad I had called Dawn. She was a wealth of information and shed a lot of light on another suspect.

Valerie Young.

CHAPTER ELEVEN

"Fifi, do you think that fight we heard between Valerie and Nadine earlier was about the contract?" I snuggled her tighter on our way back to the camper and recalled the loud argument we'd heard when we'd walked past their camper earlier.

The night clouds had thickened under the heavy snowfall, making the campground dark and silent. The bare trees howled in the wind that'd swept down from the Daniel Boone National Park and rushed across the campground.

"If you think about it," I talked to Fifi like she was my co-sleuth. "Nadine is probably Valerie's big client. Which makes me want to look her up to see who else she represents." I was starting to come up with ideas, though my stomach tugged at me, telling me to just let Hank do his job.

That wasn't going to be possible if he thought Abby Fawn - sweet Abby Fawn, of all people - could kill someone. I couldn't let that thought cross my mind.

"If Nadine decided to go in a different direction in her career and not keep Valerie as her agent, wouldn't that hurt Valerie's income?" I wasn't sure how this whole agent and writer thing worked, but I was good at getting to the bottom of things. Getting to the bottom of Valerie Young's life was now a priority.

"Psst."

I stopped dead in my tracks. My heart's pace picked up. My palms started to sweat even though my fingers were chilled to the bone. Someone was here. I gulped and tried not to move. Was Valerie here to finish me off?

"Pssssst."

"I've got a gun," I said with a trembling voice. "I'm not scared to use it."

"For heaven's sake, you don't have a gun." Mary Elizabeth's voice broke through the cold silence. "Act like you've got some sense, May-bell-ine."

"Mary Elizabeth," I sighed with relief. "Where are you?" I asked and looked around in the dark.

"Right over here." She stepped out from behind a camper. Her silhouette was barely visible in the darkness.

"What on earth are you doing out here?" I asked.

"I saw the lights on at the office and I couldn't sleep with a killer on the loose. I mean, have you seen all those scary movies about camping and killers?" she asked.

"I have not. There's not a killer on the loose." At least I didn't think there was until now. "Come on. Come back to my RV and get warm."

"May-bell-line, I think we've reached a new level in our mother and daughter relationship." No amount of darkness would dull those bright white teeth behind that big ol' smile of hers.

Even though she was dressed for the Antarctic in her full-length fur coat and fur hat, the offer I made her even surprised me.

"What were you doing in the office at this time of the night?" She asked and took Fifi from me, wrapping her up in the fur coat. Fifi licked her face.

I wondered if Fifi had that good person or bad person instinct I heard dogs had. Because she really liked Mary Elizabeth.

"When we get back to the RV, you need to keep your voice down." We hurried down through the campground. "My friend, Abby."

"The librarian?" She asked.

"Yes. In fact, I found her standing over Nadine's body with the knife dangling from her hand." It sounded so bad.

"Oh, no. Why did she kill her? And why are you harboring a killer?" Mary Elizabeth had already tried and convicted Abby without knowing the facts and that was exactly what I was afraid Hank was doing. "You found her? What about your date with hunky?"

"We were coming back from the restaurant when I noticed the library light was still on, which was weird." I pulled my keys out of my coat pocket. "We stopped and went through the unlocked door." Why was the door unlocked? There were so many questions I had for Abby. "Why do you think she did it?"

"The library light was on. The librarian didn't hide the fact that Nadine White was a fraud in her eyes in front of everyone and she was standing over the body with what I'm assuming is the murder weapon." Mary Elizabeth made it sound like Hank had a ironclad case already without interviewing anyone.

"That does sound bad." I blinked a few times before I turned to the door to unlock it. "But I know Abby and she didn't do it. Besides," I glanced at her behind me. "I found out some information about Valerie Young that would give her a clear motive to kill Nadine."

"Do tell." Mary Elizabeth might've been a full-blown southern woman, but she loved a good gossip session, which, in my opinion, was also part of being southern whether she wanted to admit it or not.

I gave her the finger to the mouth gesture when we got inside the RV. I took the opportunity to go check on Abby while Mary Elizabeth shut the door and took all the animal off of her, including Fifi.

Abby was sound asleep, and I was glad to see it. She was so much in shock that I was afraid her mind wouldn't quiet down enough for her to sleep. She was lightly snoring and lying on top of the covers. I took a quilt folded up on the dresser and gently placed it over her. There wasn't anything better than sleeping with a homemade quilt, especially during the winter.

"I hope you don't mind that I put on some coffee." Mary Elizabeth was already preparing our mugs. "Remember how we use to find each other standing over the coffeepot in the middle of the night when you'd come home from school?"

"Yes. At school I was able to stay up as late as I wanted to, but when I came back to your house for a break, you made me go to bed by ten p.m." It was funny how she thought the memory was endearing while I thought it was torture.

"It was only because I knew your brain needed rest and that beauty sleep is a real thing." She tapped around the edges of her eyes. "So is good Botox." She laughed.

"Never in a million years would I ever have thought you'd admit to Botox." I got a closer look at her. "It looks good."

"My house?" She poured the coffee into the mugs. "You said your house. It was your house too."

"I'm not going to get into all that. We are adults, so let's see where this new relationship will bring us." I grabbed one of the mugs and opened up the junk drawer to get the notebook I'd once used to write down clues in a different murder that'd taken place on one of the hiking trails around Happy Trails.

"In order to do that, I want to know why you skipped town as soon as the clock turned on your eighteenth birthday." She wasn't going to let it go.

"Let's make a deal." I knew it was going to be a deal with the devil inside of me, but I didn't want to talk about this right now. "Let me help Abby out. I need to focus all my attention on her. Then before you leave, we will sit down and talk."

"On one condition." Her voice was stern, the way I remembered it when we'd fight, and I could tell it was non-negotiable.

"What's that?" I reminded myself that I was no longer a child in the foster care system.

"You let me help you find out who really killed Nadine White." She lifted the cup of coffee to her lips and stared at me through the steam curling around her nose.

"What makes you an expert?" I pulled out the chair from the table and sat down, dragging the notebook in front of me.

"I watch those shows." She sat down in the other chair. "I always solve the mystery before Quincy does."

"Quincy? The medical examiner show?" My brows furrowed.

"What's wrong with Quincy?" She asked with an attitude.

"Nothing." I opened the notebook to a blank page. "That was a long time ago and technology has come a long way."

"There's something about good, old fashioned sleuthing. Let me prove it." She was sure of herself.

"Fine." I clicked the pen and wrote Nadine White's name at the top of a blank page.

"What's that?" She leaned on the table to see what I was writing. "Clues? I like this. Jessica Fletcher keeps all the clues in her head." She tapped her temple.

"I like to see mine. It's kinda like a puzzle." I found myself getting excited as I told her how I'd written down clues in the past and it actually helped Hank figure out who the real killer was. "Just like with those cases, I have that same gut feeling that Abby didn't do it."

"What about Valerie Young? You mentioned her earlier?" She asked and took sips of her coffee.

I told her about how Fifi and I overheard the arguing from their camper.

"Though I couldn't distinguish Nadine's voice because it was muffled, it was clearly Valerie yelling." I made bullet points under Valerie's name and wrote down key points about the argument I'd overheard. "I was at the office because everyone who rents from me has to fill out a next of kin form in case they get hurt on a trail or something. Nadine White listed Dawn Gentry, her best friend. Get this." I wrote Dembrowski next to White. "Nadine's real last name isn't White. Her real name is Nadine Dembrowski."

"That doesn't surprise me. A lot of authors use pen names." Mary Elizabeth sounded sure of herself.

"Dawn told me Nadine was going to cut out the middleman in negotiating her deals, which means she's getting rid of Valerie as her agent." I wrote down Dawn's name and some of the key points she told me about what Nadine had told her.

"This gives Valerie a clear motive. The average agent gets fifteen percent of the author's royalties." Mary Elizabeth pulled out her cell phone and started to punch away on it. "And it's for life. Unless the author takes the agent to court to break the contract, but that rarely happens."

"How on earth do you know all this?" I asked.

"Real Housewives." She nodded. "All those girls get book contracts and they always complain about their agents getting so much money."

I was taken back at how much she knew.

"According to Nadine White's contract with her publisher for *Cozy Romance in Christmas*, she received a three million dollar advance. She turned the phone around and showed me a website.

"Is that fake news?" I had to ask because it wasn't a three million dollar book.

"No. This is a site called Publisher's Marketplace. They post all the deals made in the publishing world with agents." She punched away. "What's fifteen percent of three million?'

"Valerie Young would make that much?" My jaw dropped. "No wonder she was yelling and screaming at Nadine. I wonder if Nadine had told her she was cutting her out. When Nadine left to take Abby the basket, it would have been the perfect time for Valerie to set up Abby. After all, like you said, everyone heard Abby after she found out Nadine White had a ghost writer."

"Perfect motive. Money. That's what Columbo always said." Mary Elizabeth's right brow rose, her lips puckered. "MeTV is my second favorite channel."

She yammered on about the channel while I pretended to listen.

Instead, I wrote down all the reasons why Valerie Young should be looked at as a suspect.

I drew a long line across the page and wrote ten p.m. about a quarter of the way down with a vertical line.

"What's that?" Mary Elizabeth asked.

"A timeline." I pointed to the time. "Hank and I stopped at the library at ten p.m. That's when we found Abby standing over Nadine's body." Underneath the timeline, I drew another one with Nadine's name, another one with Abby's name, and a third one with Valerie's name. "We need to snoop around and figure out where these three people were during the hours leading up to when we found them."

"I get it." She snapped her fingers. "If there's a gap and no one can account for where they were, then we just might have a killer."

"Let's hope and pray Abby has a tight alibi." I gnawed at my lip as I tried to think back to when I'd talked to Abby earlier in the day to recall if she'd said anything about what she was doing that night.

The knock on the door made me jump, Mary Elizabeth gasp, and Fifi bark.

"Who could that be at this hour?" Mary Elizabeth's question caused me to look at the clock. It was two a.m.

"I bet it's Hank." I got up and opened the door, fully expecting to see him standing there since it was probably about time he'd clear the crime scene. He was pretty quick and thorough. "Can I help you?"

I asked the woman standing at the camper door, shivering.

"I'm Dawn Gentry, Nadine's best friend." Her teeth clattered. "The sign on the office said to come here if it was after hours."

"Yeah, yeah. Come in." I held the door open for her. I had totally forgotten I was on call tonight and not Dottie. Good thing because that meant Dottie had to open the office and I still needed to get some sort of sleep. Vice versa when she was on call. "Let me get you a cup of coffee."

Dawn Gentry stood about five foot six. She tugged the knit cap off her black, pixie cut hair and vigorously rubbed her hands together. She looked like she was in her late thirties, which was where I'd place

Nadine White. She had on a pair of black skinny jeans, Doc Martin black boots, and a black leather jacket with lots of silver buckles on it.

"That'd be great." She blew into her hands. "Riding a motorcycle in this crazy weather is nearly impossible."

Fifi didn't jump around and on Dawn like she did every other visitor that came to the door. It struck me as odd.

"How did you get here so fast?" I questioned her.

"Nadine called me earlier to tell me about the fight she'd had with Valerie. I knew I had to get here as fast as I could, so I left Chicago early this morning." Her shaking hands took the coffee. She held it in her hands for a few seconds as though she were warming them up. She took a drink.

Fifi ran back to her bed and curled up.

Mary Elizabeth's mouth was gaped open and I was in shock Dawn was standing here.

"I just can't believe Nadine is dead. I mean, I've got to see it for myself." She sat in my chair without an invitation to do so. She looked around. "Can I crash here?"

"No."

"Yea."

Mary Elizabeth and I chimed in at the same time.

"Yes." I gave Mary Elizabeth a stern look. "Of course, you can stay here. But I have to warn you that one of my best friends is staying here too."

"No biggie." Dawn shrugged. "I've shared plenty of times before."

"She's actually the one the police believe killed Nadine." My words met a wide-eyed Dawn. "But I really don't think she did it."

"I thought Valerie Young. . ." Dawn looked down at my notebook in front of her. "What's this?"

"My daughter is good at solving crimes. Like Monk." I was beginning to think that Mary Elizabeth watched entirely too much TV, especially amateur sleuth shows.

"Daughter?" Dawn looked between me and Mary Elizabeth as though she were trying to see a resemblance.

I pinched a grin, holding back the urge to yell foster mother, but there was no sense in it. I'd never see Dawn again after Nadine's murderer was brought to justice and right now I wanted peace over being right.

"Anyways, it's getting late and we need to get some sleep if we are going to prove that Abby didn't kill Nadine." I grabbed my notebook and closed it. No one, not even Hank, was allowed to look at my notebook. Besides, I didn't know Dawn very well and I didn't trust her fully. At this point, everyone was a suspect.

"You'll call me first thing in the morning?" Mary Elizabeth asked, making me remember our little deal. She put on her furs.

"Yes. First thing." I guided her to the door.

"You think you're going to be okay with a stranger?" She whispered and gave a side glance to Dawn who was peeling off her clothes down to her skivvies. "She's odd."

"I'll be fine." I didn't tell her that I'd seen way worse during my ten years in New York City.

"Okay. Now call me." Mary Elizabeth slipped out of the door and into the dark night.

"You can sleep on the sofa bed." I quickly pulled the pillows off and opened it, unfolding the twin mattress hidden inside. "I'll take a captain's chair." I gathered my cell phone and took the notebook up to the front of the RV where the passenger seat would recline back enough for me to rest my eyes for a few hours.

Once I heard Dawn snoring away, I reached over and grabbed my cell phone. Swiping up, I touched the screen to turn on my flashlight. I opened the notebook to Nadine's investigation and drew a line across the page under Valerie's timeline.

"Dawn Gentry," I wrote, wondering exactly where she'd been when Nadine was murdered because if she left Chicago early this morning, which was only a little over four hours from here, where'd she been the rest of the time?

CHAPTER TWELVE

"Mae. Mae."
Faintly, I heard my name being called. The shaking made me open my eyes.

"Who's that girl sleeping on your couch?" Abby was sitting in the driver's seat of the RV.

It took me a minute to remember what'd happened the night before.

"Abby," I gasped and sat straight up. "How are you feeling?"

"I'm in shock. I only remember finding Nadine on the floor of the office with a knife stuck in her neck." She blinked back the wall of tears on her lids. "I don't even remember driving here."

"You didn't." I looked at my phone. It was seven a.m. I'd only gotten about three hours of sleep, but suddenly found myself wide awake. "The girls from The Laundry Club hurried to the library once they'd heard what was going on and Betts brought us back here."

"Who killed her? Did Hank say?" She asked, as innocent as a newborn baby.

"Honey." I reached over and touched her. "Hank thinks it was you."

"Me?" She started to sob.

"But I know you didn't do it," I whispered and looked over my shoulder at Dawn.

She was sprawled out on the twin sofa bed. One leg dangling onto the floor while the other was hiked up on the back of it. Her arms over her head. She'd slept in her black lacy underwear and bra. It was weird.

"I didn't," Abby insisted. "Why would they think that?"

"You did call her a fraud in front of everyone at the library yesterday and you were holding the knife when we found you."

She blinked a few times and stared out the windshield as if she were trying to think back into her mind.

"Abby, I need to ask you." I braced myself for either a meltdown or her going off on me. "Did you kill Nadine White?"

"No," she gasped. The lines between her brows deepened. "I just told you I didn't do it."

"Then someone has gone to great lengths to make everyone think you did." I glanced back when heard the sheets on the twin sofa bed shift. Dawn had rolled over to the side, her hiney facing out. "After Nadine dropped off your basket of goodies, what happened?"

"Basket of goodies?" Abby had a confused look on her face. "I'm not sure what you're talking about."

"Valerie said Nadine was putting together a basket of signed books for you and the library to apologize and make peace with you. When Hank and I drove through downtown on our way to the Red Barn Restaurant, we saw Nadine walking up the steps of the library with a basket in her hands." I tried to recall any details of the basket, but all I could see in my mind was her walking up and I thought about how it was the last time she'd be outside alive.

I shook the thought out of my head. Images like that weren't going to help anyone, especially Abby.

"What time was it?" she asked.

"It was a little after six." I knew the time because Hank had been right on time, but Mary Elizabeth had held us up a bit. "Hank picked me up right at six and we were stalled a little here, so it was probably between six fifteen and six thirty."

"I closed the library a little before six, so I wasn't there." Abby was certain. "I was so tired and had all my work done. The library closes at six anyways. When no one was there, I knew they didn't have time to get in and get out, so I closed up early and went home." As she talked I reached for the notebook and flipped to the timeline. "What is that?" She leaned over the middle console and looked at the paper with stark fright on her face. "You really think I killed her?"

"I don't, but Hank sure does. Don't worry. I'm going to help you." I pointed to the timelines. "Here is when we found Nadine. It was around ten." I pointed to the lines on the timeline. "We saw her a little after six p.m. She had to have been killed between six and ten, but Colonel will be able to pinpoint a more exact time."

Abby continued to stare at me blankly.

"All I need from you to help clear your name is for you to tell Hank exactly where you were and who you were with." I shrugged as though it were that simple. "You do have an alibi, right?"

"I live alone," she stated flatly.

"Yes, but you and Ty have been seeing each other, right?" I asked.

"A little here and there, but not last night." She shook her head and looked down at her fingers. The black ink from the fingerprinting was still visible. She let out a long sigh. "I forgot they fingerprinted me last night." She closed her eyes. Her nose crunched up before it flared out with a big inhale. "My goodness. I remember."

"What do you remember?" I asked.

"I remember getting fingerprinted." She didn't tell me anything I didn't already know.

"Then let's start from the beginning." I clicked the pen and pointed to her timeline with the tip. I wrote five fifty p.m. on her timeline. "Is it fair to say you left the library ten minutes early?"

"Yes. I guess." Guessing wasn't good enough, but I just went with it and wrote down that she'd left the library at that time.

"It was at least twenty minutes before Hank and I saw Nadine going up the steps. It was almost dark, and I remember there were some lights on. Did you remember turning the lights off?" I asked.

"I don't know, Mae. I have a ritual every night. That includes turning off all the computers and all the lights and making sure all the books are shelved." She was getting frustrated. "It's pretty automatic to me now."

"I'm just trying to help. You need to keep a level head. I'm your friend, but when they come at you for murder, you're going to have to be tougher than this." I had to be stern with her. She had to know what she was up against. "These are basic questions that they are going to ask you and if you waiver a bit, they will use it against you."

"I can't recall if I turned them off. I can say that I do it every night, but like I said it's automatic for me." The worry lines on her forehead deepened. "I'm sorry. I know you're trying to help me."

"No biggie." I jerked my head around when I heard a knock at the door. "Hold on. I bet it's Mary Elizabeth."

Fifi yapped when I climbed over the console into the living area of the RV. Dawn didn't budge. I wanted to cover her and her undergarments up, but didn't want to wake her.

"Good morning." I swung the door open to find Hank Sharp standing there in his official black overcoat and fancy black shoes he wore on his work days. "Hank."

"Mae," he greeted me formally. "Can I speak to Abby Fawn?"

"Sure." I offered him a slight smile while I ran my hand down my bed head full of curls.

"I'm sorry if I woke you." He stepped inside when I got out of the way of the door. "What's going on here?"

His eyes were bulging out of his head and staring at Dawn's derriere. I grabbed the blanket and threw it over her.

"What? It's hot!" Dawn was obviously not a morning person. She sat straight up. Her woman parts jiggled in her lacy bra as she rubbed her eyes, and the blanket fell around her waist. "Oh. Company." She pulled the blanket up to her chin, a slight grin on her face. "Who are you?"

"Who are you?" He asked her back.

"We can do formal introduction when you're dressed." I picked her clothes up off of my RV floor and threw them to her. I turned Hank around to face the kitchen sink. "The bathroom is that way." I pointed towards the bathroom to get Dawn scooting a little faster.

"Hi, Hank." Abby climbed over the console. "I guess you're here for me."

"I'm sorry, Abby." He looked like he was in as much pain as I was that he had to be here for this. "I'm going to need you to come to the station with me. We have to question you."

"Hank, she didn't do it." I started to plead with him. "Just let me talk to her today and we can come down later."

"You killed my best friend?" Dawn appeared out of nowhere fully dressed.

"Who are you?" Hank asked a clothed Dawn.

"I'm Dawn Gentry. I'm Nadine Debrowski's best friend." She sucked in a deep breath. "I thought for sure Valerie killed Nadine. What? Are you some crazy fan?"

"Wait a second." I stepped in. "The only thing Abby did wrong was find Nadine and pull the knife out of her neck."

"I did?" Abby didn't make matters any better. "Gosh, I did!" She gasped. "I was going to go to the diner to see Ty and I noticed the lights were still on at the library." Her eyes grew as she began to remember. "The door was unlocked. I thought maybe I was so upset from the day's events that I'd forgotten to close up. I looked around the library and nothing was out of place, so I headed back to the office where the switches are for all the lights and that's when I found Nadine's body on the floor of my office."

"Anything you say right now can be used against you." Hank had already taken out his notebook and begun scribbling on it.

"I ran over to her and saw that she was bleeding. I yanked the knife out of her neck." Abby's jaw dropped. She blinked rapidly. "I heard something." She looked down at the ground. Her eyes darted back and forth. "I heard something behind me and then some footsteps."

"What did you hear?" I asked wondering if it was a clue that someone else was in the library. "Someone was in there. The killer."

"Okay. I have to stop this," Hank interrupted.

"But she's remembering for the first time." I tried to stop him.

"Abby, can you please come with me?" He asked her nicely. "I don't want to cuff you."

"Are you arresting her?" I asked.

"You better arrest her." Dawn stuck her hands on her thin hips. "Or I'll get someone who will and bring this murderer to justice."

"I'm not a murderer!" Abby yelled and began to sob. "I didn't kill her," her voice trailed off.

"Let's just go down to the station and sort out some particulars," Hank suggested. But he and I both knew he was going to charge her with Nadine's death.

"Okay." Abby conceded.

I stomped around Hank, grabbed Abby's coat, and took her cell phone off the charger, giving them to her.

"I'll call a lawyer." I helped her get her arm through the sleeve. "Don't say a word and I mean it. If you have to bite your tongue while they interrogate you, do it. Don't say a word," I warned her again.

"Okay." She nodded and took a deep swallow.

Hank gave Dawn another good, hard look before he followed Abby out of the RV.

"Hank," I called after him and stood on the step, shivering. "You know deep down she didn't do this."

"Mae, the evidence speaks for itself." He was always by the book. "I'm sorry."

My breath and the cold air mixed together in puffs of smoke as I took several deep breaths in and out of my nose as I watched them drive off.

Fifi was dancing around my feet to get out of the RV to do her morning business.

"Let me get my coat." I took a few steps in and grabbed my coat off the hook and my phone off the counter.

Fifi darted out and I shut the door behind us.

Scrolling through my contacts, I had to find the one person I knew could help us. Ava Grandy.

"Mae West." Her voice dripped with sarcasm. "I didn't think I'd be hearing from you again. Especially in this year."

"Ava, I need your help." I wished I didn't have to call her. After my ex-husband destroyed her family, I was sure she didn't want anything to do with me. "A friend of mine is in jail. She's being accused of a murder she didn't commit. She needs you. I need you."

There were a few moments of silence.

"Fine," she finally answered, sending some relief to my soul. "Normal Police Station?"

"Yes. Thank you, thank you," was all I could say.

"I'll be there this morning." She had to drive down to Normal from Lexington, where she lived. "Tell her not to say a word."

"Don't worry. I did." I was glad I thought to tell Abby that before she left because she was so honest she'd just spill her guts without thinking how any of it sounded to any cop. Even worse, to Hank Sharp, who was always assessing what everyone said.

"Mae, did she do it? Really?"

"No. I think she was set up, but the evidence is really good against her. Me and Hank found her standing over the body with the murder weapon." It looked as bad as it sounded.

"Don't tell me this is that famous author?" She asked. I was silent. "Good grief. It's all over the news. I'll be there as soon as I can."

CHAPTER THIRTEEN

"What are we going to do now?" Dawn was sitting at my small kitchen table, drinking a cup of coffee. She was waiting for me to get dressed.

"I'm going to call Hank to see if they are finished with Nadine's camper, so I can get you over there to stay while you are here." I pulled my curly hair back into a low ponytail. There was no time to fool with it today. I had to get in touch with the girls from The Laundry Club and call an emergency meeting. "Then, I have to work."

After Hank had taken Abby to the station with him, other officers had showed up at the campground to go through Nadine's camper. The car wasn't there, and I wondered if Valerie had skipped town. The police were still over there.

"What is your plan?" I asked her, making sure she knew I wasn't going to be stuck with her. There was something odd about her and my gut tugged when I went to tell her something but stopped. That was a sign for me to just let this thing play out with her. My gut was never wrong. Plus, Fifi was still standoffish with her.

"I'm going to go to the morgue. First thing." She patted her shin to try to get Fifi to come to her, but gave up after a couple of tries.

"You're going to drive that motorcycle around?" I asked.

"It's all I got." She shrugged. "I might call an Uber or something."

"Let me see if I can get you a ride into town." Even though I didn't trust her, it wasn't in my nature to let her drive on the dangerous roads. It was slick out there. "I can always get you a ride back."

"Thanks. I noticed everything is pretty close together, so I can walk around. No biggie." She sent my inner alarm off.

When I called her, she sounded asleep. It was also dark out. When did she see downtown in the light? There was something that didn't feel right about this girl.

"Bobby Ray, can I ask you a favor?" I called him since I knew he'd be driving into downtown where the morgue was located, along with all the other businesses. "I need you to drop someone off at the morgue on your way to work."

Bobby Ray told me that Mary Elizabeth had kept him up half the night gabbing on and on about the murder and how she was going to help me solve it. Then he agreed to take Dawn. The best news was that Mary Elizabeth was still sound asleep, which meant the faster I got out of the campground, the better.

It was perfect timing too. Bobby Ray was leaving right then. Once he and Dawn were off, I gave Fifi some kibble along with some treats to hold her over for a few hours.

Quickly, I sent a text to the girls at The Laundry Club, telling them to meet me as soon as possible to discuss Abby's situation. With my notebook in hand, I was out the door in no time.

Dottie texted back to let her know what was going on when we found something out since she had to work at the Happy Trails office this morning. Everyone was going to need time to get ready and it would take even some more time to get to the laundromat driving in the snow.

We were going to need something to wake us up besides coffee and that meant a good sweet treat from The Cookie Crumble Bakery. It was exactly what we needed to get our sleuthing caps on and get our little investigation underway.

"Mae, good morning," Christine Watson, owner of the Cookie

Crumble Bakery, greeted me as soon as I walked in the door. Her bubbly personality was infectious. It was her calling to bake donuts and all the other fun pastries because she put people in happy moods first thing in the morning when they came in to get their morning treat. "Did you try those candy cane donuts I sent over this morning?"

"I didn't." I eyeballed the delish looking pastry that was festive to look at.

"Here. Try a sample." Christine pointed to a silver platter of samples on top of one of the bakery counters.

The little toothpicks stuck in them were a mix of red, and green, and white, all the colors of Christmas. It was the small touches that made everything in all of Normal's shops feel so special.

"Gosh. This is amazing." I had to refrain from grabbing all the samples. "You are so good."

"I think it's because I use as many local ingredients as I can from farmers in the area." There was a look of satisfaction on her face. She was so humble and that was one of her most endearing qualities. "I get all my eggs and dairy from the dairy farm off Route 44." She continued to tell me other places where she got her ingredients, but my taste buds were so caught up in the mix of peppermint and sweet glaze, my mind just couldn't process her words.

"I'd love to have a few to take over to the gals at The Laundry Club this morning." I walked down the glass counter. My mouth watered at the amazing creations Christine made. "And I'd love it if I could get you to make me enough for the Christmas Dinner at the Campground. About one hundred in total."

She didn't make just any donuts. She used her artistic ability to create different designs. She wasn't afraid to stack different textures on top of each other.

"I'll take a couple of those s'mores too." The drizzled chocolate over crumbled graham crackers and marshmallows on top of a glazed donut was calling my name and my thighs. I couldn't tell if she was processing my request for her to cater the donuts for the dinner. "The donuts would be a great dessert for the Christmas dinner."

"I'd love to make them for free, if you can supply all the dairy needed." She snapped a glove from the box and put it on her hand. "You can tell Kelli Sergeant how many you want me to make and she'll get all the ingredients ready for you."

"Kelly Sergeant?" I questioned.

Even though I'd been living in Normal for a few months now, I still didn't know everyone who called Normal home. I pretty much stuck to the campground and my girlfriends at the Laundry Club. I knew there were a lot of shops and stores out of the downtown area that I'd yet to explore, and the Milkery Dairy Farm was one of them.

"Yes. She's the owner of the Milkery." Christine referred to it by its nickname. "There's a card in one of the holders over there next to the cash register."

I walked over there and looked at all the business cards Christine let locals put there for marketing.

"The Milkery Dairy Farm," I said with a smile and picked up the white card with big black blotches all over it that were supposed to represent cow spots. It was cute.

"I'm sorry to hear about the famous author staying at the campground. It's a shame too. I was looking forward to getting to know her better." Christine had a Cookie Crumble Bakery to-go box in one hand and a gloved hand putting my goodies in it with the other.

"You knew her?" I asked, thinking it was strange she mentioned getting to know her better.

"Yesterday, someone from her publishing team came in and got a couple of maple cream long johns. They said she was going to love them, and I gave her my card. She also asked if I did deliveries." She flipped the sides of the cardboard down on the box and peeled off a Cookie Crumble Bakery logo sticker to seal it. "Since I have my sister deliver your donuts each morning, I didn't see a problem making a special delivery to her. Especially if she liked them and told her readers about them." She removed the glove from her hand and tapped her temple. "It's all about the marketing."

"Don't I know. Abby Fawn. . ." I was going to say that Abby was instrumental in getting Happy Trails Campground as popular as it'd become with all her marketing, but I wondered when Valerie Young had come in here when I didn't see her leave Nadine's side until after their blow up. According to my timeline, that was later in the day, before my six p.m. date with Hank. "The person who came in here." I held my hand above my head. "Was she about this tall, lanky, with dishwater brown hair? Sorta greasy?"

"No." Christine shook her head and handed me the box over the bakery counter. "She had the cutest black pixie cut."

"What time was this?" I asked knowing it had to be Dawn.

"Around noonish. I know that because I was getting ready to take some of the older donuts out of the case. I distribute them to the homeless shelter, the police station, and the fire department so they don't go to waste." She smiled, causing the freckles across her nose to spread along her cheeks. "I do that at lunchtime, so I can put out freshly baked pastries and pies out for the lunch crowd. That's when I sell the most pies and cakes. You know," she flip flopped her hand in the air, "customers like to have them for dessert after supper."

"Yeah." I wasn't fully listening to her. I took the notebook out of my purse to write this down under Dawn's timeline. "Tell me again what she said."

I scribbled as Christine recalled her interaction with Dawn. It had to be Dawn. She had described her to a tee, including the motorcycle.

"I even told her I'd deliver them since she was driving that motorcycle." She laughed. "Who ever thought of driving a motorcycle in the snow? I told her she could go to Grassel's Garage to see if Joel had a car she could rent."

"What did she say?" I asked.

"She said she didn't plan on being in town long and left." Christine's interaction with Dawn had me on high alert. Why didn't she tell me? What was Dawn Gentry hiding?

After I paid Christine for the donuts, I decided to walk down to The Laundry Club. There was no sense in trying to find a cleared parking spot since I already had one and the Laundry Club was only a short walk down Main Street.

The snow didn't seem to bother the tourists. I'd never known people to love hiking so much that they'd strap on snow shoes along with their hiking gear to find the perfect trails in this sort of weather. They were lucky the rangers hadn't closed down the park since the snowfall hadn't let up since yesterday morning.

The lampposts along Main Street had garland wrapped around them and the loveliest poinsettias in hanging baskets added the perfect pop of color against the snow. Each hanging basket sported the logo of the Sweet Smell Flower Shop, a perfect way to advertise. I waved at Gert Hobson, the owner of The Trails Coffee Shop, when I noticed she was in the display window adding the finishing touches to the coffee mug Christmas tree she'd cleverly crafted. It was so cute.

The Trails Coffee Shop was another local shop I had an agreement with for Happy Trails Campground. Gert supplied the coffee that was the perfect accompaniment to Christine's donuts. It was a good way to promote their business and when I passed, I noticed a couple of my hikers inside enjoying a steaming cup of something Gert had to offer.

The Smelly Dog Groomer had their grooming tables all lined up. I had to get Fifi in there for her Christmas haircut and nails. Ethel Biddle tapped on the window to get my attention. Rosco, Fifi's boyfriend and father of her pups, was sitting next to her. Ethel gave me the telephone sign up to her ear to tell me to call her. She'd been driving me crazy about setting up a play date for the lovebirds...er...love dogs. I nodded and smiled, heading right past Cute-icles. I tried not to make eye contact with Helen Ryle, who was yammering away at a client sitting in the stylist's chair, snipping off hair as fast as she talked.

Unfortunately, I wasn't quick enough. Helen pointed to her own orange hair, her bejeweled smock glistening more than the Christmas ornaments she had dangling from the ceiling all over the salon. That woman had more glitter on those ornaments than her nail techs were putting on their clients' Christmas nails. Glitter and big hair had never gone out of style in Normal.

Downtown was very interesting. Each shop had had its own outdoor courtyard. Today each shop owner had a Christmas tree decorated to match their store's theme, but during the warmer months, each shop had neat little activities on a daily basis. It was fun to walk around Main Street when you needed something to do.

I glanced across the street at the Tough Nickel Thrift Shop and Deter's Feed-N-Seed. Both looked busy. I was glad the snow didn't stop the tourists from coming. But I wondered if the news about Nadine White, once it got out, would change that.

"Where've you been?" Queenie tapped her watch after I pushed through the door at the Laundry Club. She tapped the glass globe in front of her. It was one of those electric globes that sent little lightning bolts to the surface of the glass when you touched it. She was so odd. She liked to scare patrons of the laundromat by acting like she could tell their futures. Her neon green headband and matching neon green bodysuit didn't help matters.

"What on earth do you have on?" I shook my head as I walked past her to take the donuts back to the table with the half-finished Christmas puzzle Betts was working on.

"I like to wear my Jazzercise one piece as long johns and I don't look too bad for an old brood." She slid her hands over the sides of her body and did a little shimmy, following along behind me. "So, I can afford to eat one of those donuts in the Cookie Crumble Bakery box you got there."

"I'm glad I stopped by because Christine gave me some new information." I sat the box down and took the notebook out of my bag.

"I stopped by to see Abby on my way in. Lester is going to see her this morning too." Betts picked one of the candy cane donuts and Queenie took one of the s'mores. "Hank said she wasn't talking."

"Good. I've got Ava Grandy coming to see her this morning. Do you know Colonel Holz?" I asked Betts since she knew everyone in town.

"Yes. He's a member of the congregation," she said under a muffled mouthful of donut. "If you came to church every once in a while, you'd know him too." She couldn't let that one go without a little dig. "I'm guessing you want to go talk to him about the case."

"Yeah. I've got a few questions about the autopsy." I was starting to second guess if the knife was the only murder weapon.

"What about it? It seems pretty clear she died from the neck wound," Queenie said.

"By the looks of it, but I'm wondering if she were poisoned by a donut." My words made the two of them look at their half-eaten sweet treats and then at each other.

Both shrugged and kept eating.

I opened the notebook to the timeline and notes I'd made on the case and told them about Dawn Gentry coming into town fairly quickly after I called her as the Nadine's next of kin. They were more interested in Nadine's real last name than my overnight guest. But when I mentioned she'd been in town longer than she'd disclosed to me and how she'd gotten donuts around noon, that got their attention.

"What's her name?" Betts took out her phone and typed it in as I rattled it off. "She lives in Chicago and she's single. She's a bartender."

"How do you know all that?" I asked.

"You really need to get on Facebook." She handed me her phone. "You can learn a lot about someone on there."

I scrolled through Dawn's Facebook while they finished eating and the coffeepot Betts brewed finished percolating. There were a few photos of Dawn and Nadine together. There were a couple of comments under a photo from one of Nadine's book signings.

"I'm thrilled to see you made up," I read out loud. "This was just a couple of months ago at the release party of *Cozy Romance in Christmas*. I wonder what this was about."

I clicked on the person who made the comment and hit the message button.

"What are you doing?" Betts grabbed her phone back.

"I was sending this person a message. I want to know what he is talking about." I reached for her phone again.

"Get your own Facebook." Betts's eyes lowered. "I'm not letting you use mine to investigate. It's the church's account. Besides, Lester thinks we need to let the police handle it."

"If that was the case, Hank would already have Abby in the electric chair for killing Nadine." I knew something was up with Dawn. There had to be a motive.

"What can we do to help?" Queenie asked.

"I'm going to go right over there and join Facebook. If I send you a screenshot of Dawn's profile photo you can take the list of all the people from Nadine's library talk and see if they recognize Dawn." I knew it was a long shot, and it'd take time, but it sure would help me out. "You did say that everyone at the library bought Tupperware from Abby, right?"

"They did, and I can stop by to see Abby. Kill two birds with one stone. See how she's doing and ask her where the list is." Queenie stood up. She did some sort of stretch and trotted off towards the computer Betts kept for the customers of The Laundry Club to use. "I'll get you started on Facebook. I'll make one for Happy Trails too."

I wanted to protest both, but I let her.

"Now, back to Colonel." I turned to Betts. "How quick do you think you could get me to see him?"

"I guess we could go now. I know he works first thing in the morning." She took another donut and handed me one.

"Perfect," I said biting into the donut, talking about it and the fact that Betts could get me to see the Colonel ASAP.

CHAPTER FOURTEEN

"This is all sorts of creepy," I said to Betts as we took the freight elevator that just so happened to be big enough for a church cart to carry a dead body to the freezing cold basement of the only emergency clinic in Normal.

"The morgue is in the basement, so yeah. It's creepy." Betts didn't seem to be as uncomfortable as I was as I fidgeted in my skin. "Here we are."

The doors opened onto a long hallway with concrete flooring, making it even more eerie. The sound of the elevator ding echoed off the walls, creating goosebumps all over my arms.

"You coming or not?" Betts had noticed my hesitation when I didn't get off the elevator behind her. She held the box of leftover donuts in her hands, which I found odd.

The sound of our footsteps was the only sound around us as we made our way down to the end of the hall. There was a big silver button on the wall that we had to push to open the steel doors.

"Colonel? It's Betts." We stood in the entrance of what appeared to be an office.

Colonel's face appeared in the small round window in another set of double steel doors. He smiled when he made eye contact with Betts.

"Betts, to what do I owe the pleasure?" He peeled the long yellow gloves that reached to his elbows off before he reached out to pat her on the arm.

"This is my friend Mae West." She introduced me.

"Ah, the famous Mae West. Owner of Happy Trails Campground." He bowed. "Part-time sleuth." He lifted his brows and gave me the side-eye.

"So you've heard about me?" I asked with a smile.

"I've been warned that you might stop by. It wasn't with this case, but a previous one. Now, what are you snooping around about?" The corners of his mouth turned up.

"Since you asked, you know that it appears as if Nadine White, um, Dembrowski's cause of death was a stab wound to the neck." Here was my conspiracy theory. "I'm wondering if that was a secondary wound and maybe poison killed her."

"Since I've just started to work on the victim, I can tell you that I've only gotten to the stab wound." He grabbed a chart off of his desk and pulled the glasses down off of his bald head. "Without saying anything to hurt Hank Sharp's investigation, and honoring my commitment to Betts and her friendship, I will tell you that the blood around the stab wound doesn't correspond with when the rigor mortis set in, which I'm placing at around 8 p.m."

"So, you can confirm that something else killed her?" I asked.

"I'm not confirming anything until I talk to Hank first." His stomach grumbled. His eyes shifted to the box Betts held.

"Here." I took the box. "We brought you some donuts."

"Betts," he winked. "You know my weakness."

"I've never stopped by without bringing you a sweet treat." Betts had known all along the Colonel loved donuts and I loved that she had used them to get what we wanted.

Colonel took the box and laid the file on the desk. He patted the file.

"I'm going to grab my coffee. It might be a few minutes." He gave me a sly smile. One that told me he wasn't giving me permission to look in the file he'd left behind, but he didn't try to hide the file either.

Once he was through the door, Betts grabbed the file.

"Where's your cell?" She asked me in a hurried voice. "You need to take pictures of this quickly."

"You are awful, and I love it!" I was excited to have Betts on my side with this one. She was just as invested in getting Abby out of jail and bringing the real killer to justice as I was.

"Are you done?" He's coming back.

"Yes." I flipped the file closed with one hand and put my phone back in my pocket with the other. "I noticed you didn't get your hands dirty."

"That's for you to do. I just said I knew Colonel." Betts wasn't dumb. She knew exactly how to keep her squeaky clean image as the preacher's wife.

"Now. Where are those donuts?" Colonel didn't give us a second glance. His eyes were focused on the Cookie Crumble Bakery box. "You know, Christine is a whiz at this." He took one of the s'more donuts out of the box and rotated it, looking at it from all angles. "There's something to be said about using fresh ingredients. Did you know she buys as many local ingredients as she can from local farmers and the farmer's market?"

"I can tell a store-bought chicken egg in a minute." I smiled, lying through my teeth. "That's why I love this town so much. We support each other. That's what we're doing with Abby Fawn." I gestured between me and Abby. "I truly don't think she did it and if what you said about the blood from the neck . . ."

"What did you say?" Hank Sharp stood behind us. His green eyes had a hint of wonder in them.

"You were right." Colonel pushed the box across the desk with his free hand. "She even brought me some good donuts."

"Mae." The sound of my name coming out of Hank's mouth was filled with more disappointment than romance like before he kissed me the other night. "Betts, I'm shocked to see you here."

"I'm just here to say hello to Colonel and thank him for his generous offering during last Sunday's collection." Betts wasn't fooling anyone, even though she'd fully convinced herself she had.

"Mmmhhhh." Hank took one of the donuts from the box. "Mae, can I see you in the hall?"

"Umm. . .okay." I walked past him with my chin held high. Once we were outside and the door was shut behind us, I told him what I thought, "This is a free country Hank Sharp. You and no one can't tell me that I can't come visit the morgue or the coroner. It's my tax dollars and my vote that put him in this building and I can darn well go anywhere I please."

"You're right." He nodded and took a bite of the donut.

"I'm what?" I asked. My jaw dropped, but my head said that something wasn't right. There was no way Hank Sharp just told me I was right.

"I said, you're right. You do have a right to be here and check out what your tax dollars go towards, but." Here it came. " You don't have the right to snoop into an official investigation."

"You'd think that after three other crimes," I jabbed my finger in the air, "Make that three other murders, that you'd get used to me trying to help you figure this out."

"What is it that makes you so drawn to murder?" He asked a very good question that I should explore. Maybe with a therapist or something.

That thought aside, I retorted, "Because I love this town and I want to make sure the whole world gets to know how we care for each other. We support each other and that's why we have such amazing shops and wonderful people that want the tourists to come explore." I pointed to his donut. "You want to know why Christine's donuts taste so good?"

"Sugar?" He asked and stuffed the rest of it in his mouth.

"No. The fact that she uses fresh ingredients from local farms. That's what it is. Real love is baked into all that." I circled my finger around his lips before I used the pad of my finger to swipe off the little bit of chocolate that'd dripped down on his chin.

"How about supper tonight?" The corner of Hank's lip curled up. "You're so cute when you get all huffy and puffy mad. Like an old wet hen."

"Hank Sharp, I don't like to be compared to an old wet hen." My shoulders drooped as a big sigh left my body. "Supper is good. I need to eat."

"And. . ." He hesitated as though he were deciding whether or not to tell me something. "I'm not sure why, but people love to talk to you. If you do hear anything about the case, I'm sure you'll tell me."

"Are you asking me to snoop?" I asked. "Because you know that Abby Fawn didn't do this."

"Ava Grady said you sent her down here." He turned all serious again. "From the phone call I got from Colonel this morning, the initial autopsy report says there was a primary cause of death and the stab wound was secondary."

"Like the killer was making sure they'd gotten the job done." The thought that someone had such hatred towards someone else sent chills all over my body.

"I'm not sure, but I've got a theory." Hank took a couple of steps towards the door.

"What is your theory?" I asked.

He turned shy of the door and glanced at me over his shoulder.

"That, you don't need to know. I'm the detective, you're the ears I need in the community and around the campground." He made the line very clear. "Nobody in the campground wants to talk to me."

I followed behind him as he headed back into the room. Betts and Colonel were discussing some sort of theological issue I had no knowledge of but stopped when we were all present.

"Are you ready?" Colonel asked Hank and picked up Nadine's file.

"Yep." Hank gave a hard nod. "Mae, I'll see you tonight."

"Mae," Betts gushed after there was plenty of time for Colonel and Hank to leave the room and head back into the morgue to discuss whatever it was Colonel had discovered. "You've got a boyfriend. And you said it was just a date."

"It was a date," I reminded her. "But a dead body interrupted what could've been a really good night. First one I would have had in a long time."

"It sounds like it didn't interrupt anything." Betts curled her arm in the crook of mine as we made our way back to the elevator.

This time, I wasn't nervous because we were going up and getting out of there.

"Now what?" She asked, dropping me back off at the Cookie Crumble Bakery where I'd left my car.

"I'm going to get a Facebook account and check out what this guy meant about Dawn's photo with Nadine." I didn't want to get on social media, but it was time. Especially if I wanted to figure out just who Dawn was and how to get her on the suspect list.

"I'll go and see Abby. Make sure everything is okay. I'll see if she remembers anything else." Betts waved me off.

I hurried to my car, dodging more big flakes of snow. There were a lot of snow squalls, where the snow would stop for a brief time before it fell again, but in very large quantities. It was something that wasn't unusual for this area, which made me take it extra slow on the way back to the campground.

By the time I made it back, it was lunchtime and I could smell the chili Dottie had cooked in the large kettle pot on the outside fire pit. I'd initially had it built for the nightly cookouts the campers enjoyed so much during the warmer weather.

Around suppertime, each camper that wanted to participate would build up their outdoor firepit and get it going with something tasty, making enough for everyone to come around and have some. By the time you made it around to each camper, you'd had a full meal. That turned into me making the main meal over the big fire pit and something the entire town turned out for.

We had desserts out the ying-yang along with any sort of drink, including cocktails, you could imagine. The meats, vegetables and dairy were fresh from the farm, which reminded me of the Cookie Crumble Bakery and Dawn Gentry.

Dottie was sitting at her desk with her feet propped up, looking through one of them trashy celebrity magazines.

"Looky here." She flipped the pages taut and folded the magazine in half. She tapped the article she wanted me to read. "It's the account of that photographer who had a fight with Nadine White. I bet he killed her."

"Let me see that." I hurried over to her, shedding my coat as I went.

"According to this, Nadine White got a restraining order against this photographer. Her photos brought him tons of money, making her his cash cow."

"And he could have killed her to get revenge." I grabbed my notebook out of my purse and made another timeline below Dawn's. "Does it say what his name is?" I sat down at my desk.

"Mmmhmmm…" Dottie pulled her eye readers off the top of her head and put them on. She lifted her chin and drew her eyes down her nose. "Some feller by the name of Reed Fowler."

"Reed Fowler," I repeated and wrote his name down along the line. "Now I have three suspects other than Abby."

Things were looking a little better and I couldn't wait to tell Hank about it tonight.

"Who?" Dottie dragged her feet off the desk and took her readers off.

"I've got Valerie Young because Nadine White was going to take her income away by firing her as her agent." I quickly told Dottie how I'd overheard Valerie and Nadine yelling when Fifi and I were walking home.

"Money can be so bad." Dottie tsked. "It brings out the evil in people."

"Then there's Dawn Gentry." I'd completely forgotten I'd not told Dottie about the name listed as Nadine's contact person on the rental contract. "What do you think about that?" I asked after I told Dottie all the sketchy stuff Dawn had done since she'd been in town. "I'm going to open a Facebook account, so I can dig deeper into that photograph."

I shook the mouse hooked up to the computer and brought the blank screen to life.

Dottie looked over my shoulder with her readers back on the edge of her nose.

"Put your email there." She pointed out. "Right there is a password."

"Dottie," I looked at her out of the corner of my eye. "Do you want to do this?"

"I want to make one for Happy Trails, but you didn't want to do that." She was good at reminding me of things I'd been opposed to once the campground started to take off. "I told you that millennials have got this spirit to camp, glamp, and hike. They are begging for a place like Happy Trails."

"Fine." I pushed my chair back. "Have at it."

"Now you're talking about killing two birds with one stone. We get business, while you can use it to snoop around." She was able to talk and get the Happy Trails Facebook page up in no time.

We talked about Abby and how we needed to figure out if she had an alibi, which made me wonder if she had been able to remember anything for either Ava or Betts. Neither of them had called me, and I didn't want to bug them, so I'd keep trying to find new suspects. I was pretty proud of myself so far. Three would put a little bit of doubt in Hank's head.

"Also, I went to see Colonel Holz." I took out my phone. "He said Nadine's stab wound was secondary."

I scrolled through the photos of the autopsy report that I'd illegally taken.

"Where'd you get those?" Dottie was caught off guard with the photos.

"If I told you, I'd have to kill you." I teased and decided it was best for her not to know. "It doesn't matter. What matters is that Abby didn't kill her. It was something else, but he wouldn't tell me what."

"Let me see that." She reached for the phone. Her eyes squinted behind the readers as she used the tips of her fingers to make the photos bigger and smaller. Drawing them together and then apart. "It looks like she had been poisoned."

"I knew it!" I grabbed the notebook. "I think Dawn Gentry poisoned the donuts and gave one to Nadine."

"Even if she did poison her, how did she get poison?" Dottie asked, looking up over the top of her glasses at me.

"I don't know. But it's a good theory anyways. Good enough for me to tell Hank and he can do his detectiving to find out." I recorded the poisoning theory in my notebook.

"Is detectiving a word?" Dottie smiled and went back to typing on the computer. "I'll use the pretty lake photo from the tiki summer party we had." She was getting into building the Facebook page.

"Can I look around and let you finish that up in a minute?" I asked.

"Why are you in such a hurry? Got a date?" She snickered. "One without a dead body?" She laughed louder.

"Yes. Yes, I do. It's a do-over date. And without a dead body." I flipped the notebook closed and looked over her shoulder at the screen. "Look up Dawn Gentry," I told her. "On her page, you'll find a photo of her and Nadine."

I watched her scroll down.

"There. Stop. Back," I instructed after she scrolled right on past the photo.

"It's recent too." She pointed to the date on the status, which was two weeks ago. "Here's the comment." She used the pointer of the mouse to point to the photo of the guy who'd left it. She clicked on it and brought us to his Facebook page. "Mae," she gasped. "Reed Fowler."

CHAPTER FIFTEEN

"Good girl." Dawn was sitting cross-legged on the couch when I walked back into the RV. She was having Fifi do tricks for treats for Mary Elizabeth, who was sitting next to her. Fifi had been trained to do many tricks before I had her, and she was good at it. That was one thing that made her a champion. . . until I ruined it by letting Rosco around her.

"Still here," I mumbled the observation, noticing that Fifi had warmed up to Dawn. But when Dawn looked at me, her eyes were puffy and red.

"Me or her?" Mary Elizabeth asked.

"Are you okay?" I took a good look at Dawn before I went into the rage about how I knew she was friends with Reed Fowler, the paparazzi that'd followed Dawn to Normal.

"She didn't kill Nadine." Mary Elizabeth chirped up, all while rubbing the back of Dawn's back, comforting her.

"No. I'm not okay. My best friend is dead. Remember?" She shifted, pushing her legs out in front of her and curling Fifi in her arms. As though she had just processed with Mary Elizabeth had said, she retorted, "Did you just say I didn't kill Nadine? Of course, I didn't kill her. I'm just not doing well with this. No one will help me. I've called the police and I called that detective. No one will tell me anything. I need to go see her."

"We've talked." Mary Elizabeth pushed Dawn's legs together. "Honey, southern ladies don't sit with their legs spread as wide as Texas."

"You're giving her lessons in manners?" I looked at Mary Elizabeth in disbelief. "Listen, I know that you lied to me." I tugged my coat off and hung it up. I took my notebook out of my purse and sat down at the table. "You acted as though you were in Chicago when I called you this morning. Then you told me that you were on your way. You showed up fast. Then I found out you'd gone to the Cookie Crumble Bakery and got donuts."

"I never once told you I was in Chicago. How did you know I live in Chicago?" Dawn asked me with a scowl on her face.

"Her boyfriend probably told her." Mary Elizabeth shrugged. I glared at her.

"Who is your boyfriend?" Dawn had a demanding tone in her voice.

"Detective Hunky Hank." Mary Elizabeth winked.

Dawn's brows rose.

"My friend Abby Fawn is sitting in jail right now because she's suspected of killing your friend. If you think for one second that it sounds perfectly normal that you lied to me about being in town and now that we know Nadine wasn't killed by that knife and it was pois. . ." My lips snapped together.

"Spit it out." Mary Elizabeth eased to the edge of the couch. "What about the knife and something else?"

"You were going to say poison, weren't you?" Dawn sat up next to Mary Elizabeth, both of their beady eyes snapping at me.

"Did you poison the donut you gave Nadine? Did you kill her because you two didn't speak for a long time?" I questioned her like I'd seen on TV. My voice was stern. I wanted to smack my hand down on the kitchen table for effect, but I refrained since Fifi was already shaking from me yelling.

"This is nuts. Get a hold of yourself." Mary Elizabeth stood up and tugged the hem of her Christmas cardigan sweater down over the waist of her black slacks. The bells that were sewn on the collar around Rudolph's neck on her sweater jingled and his nose lit up.

Fifi growled and then barked at it.

"Tell her where you were." Mary Elizabeth drew her pointer finger from Dawn to me to get her to do it. "Go on."

"Fine. Nadine called me to come here for the holiday and help her bake. I'm a pastry chef in Chicago. Though you already probably know that." She rolled her eyes as the sarcasm dripped from her mouth. "We'd gotten in an argument years ago when she decided to take a pen name. I told her not to, but she insisted she didn't want people to know she wrote all the dirty talking stuff." She uncurled her arms and clasped her hands in her lap.

Mary Elizabeth pushed Dawn's knees together. Heaven help poor Mary Elizabeth, she was trying to keep manners alive and well while she was still kicking.

"Nadine came to Chicago to see me. We had so much fun reconnecting. She'd forgiven me after all these years and said that she did regret not keeping Dembrowski as her author name. Then she said that she was going to do this cookbook and fire Valerie. She also said that Valerie insisted she come with her here. I told her it wasn't a good idea if she was going to fire her, but she insisted she owed it to Valerie to tell her in person."

So far, everything I'd uncovered was coming together, but I still heard a few inconsistencies and wrote a few things down in my notebook.

"Tell her where you were last night at the time of Nadine's death." Mary Elizabeth tapped Dawn on the shoulder.

"I'm getting there." Dawn sat up even straighter. "Nadine made some sort of deal with Ty Randal to use his kitchen at night to test the recipes for her new cookbook." She crossed her arms over her chest. "She met with him the day she got into town. The same day Reed Fowler showed up."

"She also met with Hank to talk about security." I recalled the event well.

"Yes. She was upset about that because she gave Hank a piece of paper with the restraining order against Reed." Quickly I remembered the piece of paper Nadine White had scribbled on at the diner and handed to Hank. I'd been so focused on her flirting with him and the written words from her steamy romance novel along with the fear she might test her words out on him, I'd forgotten to ask him what was on the paper.

"A restraining order," I said with a sigh of relief. "That still doesn't clear you of killing her. You're jealous of her."

"Far from it. I don't hide behind my creations and I told her not to hide behind her talent, but she couldn't see far past her ego that I think that's what got her in trouble." She drummed her fingertips together.

"Go on." Mary Elizabeth encouraged her. "Tell her your alibi so we can put this behind us and get the real killer."

"Nadine, Ty, and I worked on a few of Nadine's ideas yesterday afternoon. Her recipes are really good. Ty even told her he'd let her serve some to his customers during her stay here, so she could get some feedback. She even took me by surprise." She smiled at the memory of her and her friend. "She got a phone call from Valerie."

This got my attention.

"Valerie had fixed up a basket of goodies to give to your local librarian, which I'm assuming is your friend, Abby. Because I met her." She swallowed so hard, I could see her throat move up and down. She licked her lips.

"Yes. You met her here." I shrugged.

"No. I saw her when Nadine took the basket to the library. But I don't think she saw my face." The lines between Dawn's eyes deepened. "Ty and I found a chemistry between us that lead to a passionate kiss. Abby let herself in the diner and saw us kissing."

You could've knocked my teeth out and I wouldn't've felt it, her words so caught me off guard and numbed me.

"Yeah. I think she was a little shocked and he was upset. I tried to tell him it was no big deal and that we weren't anything, but he said something about this town and small talk and Abby." She blinked several times. "I think he even mentioned you."

"Are you telling me you were with Ty Randal all night long and he didn't try to go find Abby?" I questioned. No wonder Abby was out of her mind and shocked all night.

"Yes, but not like you're thinking. We started drinking after Abby wouldn't talk to him. So I stayed there to make sure he was okay until we practically passed out from being so tired. When I got your call, I woke up in one of the diner's booths. He'd left me a note on the table." She pointed to her jacket. "It's in the pocket."

I hurried over to her jacket and took the note she'd referred to out of the pocket.

It was Ty's scribble. I recognized it. He said he was going to go look for Abby. He was sorry for any problems he'd caused. It was just like him to apologize for nothing he'd done. Deep down I blamed Dawn. Though. . .there were two sides to every story and Ty shouldn't have kissed Dawn.

"Ty is your alibi." I had mixed emotions about this. I was glad she hadn't killed her best friend, but I was sad on numerous levels for Abby. Now I had only two suspects. "You're going to need to tell Hank all of this. He's coming here for supper tonight."

I told her about Hank coming over so she could figure out a place to stay. I was going to make it easy on her and let her stay with Valerie in Nadine's camper since the police had cleared it, although I hadn't seen Valerie since the police station.

"What do you know about Valerie's job?" I asked. I wanted to know all the particulars to learn why Valerie Young would have a great motive to have killed Nadine.

"She's the agent. She is the one who negotiates all of Nadine's book contracts with the publisher. All the deals she made for Nadine, she got fifteen percent of each deal." Dawn rubbed her fingers and thumbs together in the money sign gesture.

"For the life of the book?" I asked.

Dawn's chin slowly lifted up and then down.

"How long is the life of a book?" I asked.

"Forever." Dawn's word had some force behind it. "Even if Nadine fired her, Valerie will still make fifteen percent of all the deals she's made so far. Nadine said that sales do drop off after a period of time, but. . ." Dawn stopped.

I had a niggling feeling she was keeping something to herself.

"What? What were you going to say?" I had to get it out of her.

"I hate to even say it out loud and I'm not going to say that it will happen with Nadine, but you see it with stars all the time." Dawn gnawed on the inside of the cheek. "Sometimes stars become more famous in death than they were living, which would mean Nadine's work so far would go up in value."

"You have to go tell Hank all of this now." It made so much sense why Valerie would kill Nadine.

"I'll take her down to see him." Mary Elizabeth walked over to get her fur coat and matching hat. "Come on, honey. We need to get this over with."

Reluctantly, Dawn stood up.

"This town is really going to hate me now. I probably broke up a good relationship." Dawn put her jacket on.

"No one is going to hate you." Mary Elizabeth looked ridiculous in that fur, but she loved it.

The pairing of Dawn and Mary Elizabeth struck me as odd, but it kept them both out of my hair.

"You can even stay with me tonight." Mary Elizabeth winked at me on her way out.

After they left, I went back over my notebook and notes, crossing Dawn off my list, but not Reed or Valerie.

I jerked the door open when I heard a knock.

"What did you forget?" I asked and found Hank standing there holding a brown bag of Chinese food.

"You forgot me, didn't you?" He looked hurt.

"Not at all." I opened the RV door wide to let him in. "Mary Elizabeth and Dawn Gentry just left. They're going to the station to give her statement."

"Yeah. I know about that." He picked up Fifi, who was yapping at him. "Let's take her for a walk before we eat so we can have some time to talk."

I wanted to run to the bathroom to get a look in the mirror but there was no sense in doing that. He'd already seen me and if I was going to put on all that snow garb, it wouldn't make a difference anyways.

"Fifi," I called her name and held up her coat. She bounced over with a wagging tail and yipped until I got the coat on her.

"Ty came to see Abby at the station. She was pretty upset," Hank told me pretty much the same thing Dawn had said.

It turned out to be a nice winter night for a stroll. The snow had stopped, and the stars were out. Along with the moon, they shined so bright they lit our way.

"I know Ty and I aren't the best of friends, but I do kinda feel for the guy." Hank reached over. His gloved hand took my gloved hand as we walked through the campground with Fifi darting in and out of the snow piles in front of us. "I got you from him," he teased.

"Stop it. He's more suited for Abby. I just don't know what happened with Dawn and him." It was so out of character for Ty. "It gives him and Dawn an alibi."

"And Abby too." He pulled me to him. "I figured I'd tell you that and you'd wrap your arms around me, giving me another one of those kisses."

"You are ruthless." I shoved him away. When our arms extended, our fingers locked together harder and I tugged him back. "Tell me how she's got an alibi?"

"Well, since you already bribed Colonel into telling you the stab was the secondary wound that happened after Nadine's heart had already stopped, Abby has an alibi for up until she found Nadine. One being the time frame she was at the diner in shock. She then ran over to the library and that's when she found Nadine. By then, Nadine had been dead an hour."

"That's when Abby was at Queenie's Jazzercise class." I dropped his hands and clapped my hands together in delight. I turned to Hank. "You're right! I could just kiss you, but. . ." I reached down and grabbed two handfuls of snow, making the biggest snow ball and throwing at him.

He ran after me with Fifi yipping on our heels. He tackled me to the ground. Both of us were giggling like we were teenagers.

"You sure are something else, Mae West." Hank's voice created an echo in the night sky as both of us fell on our backs into the fluffy snow.

"This is great snow for snow angels." I swiped my arms and legs open and closed in the deep snow to make one.

Even if I'd not figured out who'd killed Nadine White, the weight of worrying about clearing Abby was lifted off of me.

"Let's go. I'm starving." Hank and I stood up in front of our snow angels. "Aww. Cute."

"They are cute." I smiled and made a mental picture in my head of the two snow angels that looked like they were holding hands, so I wouldn't forget this time. It was adorable. And when Hank heard all my theories about Nadine's killer, he might regret he'd asked me to keep my nose and ear to the ground.

"Something on your mind?" He looked at me out of the corner of his eye as we were walking back to the RV. "Do I dare ask if it's about Nadine White?"

"Since you dare, I shall tell you," I teased hoping to cut through the tension I was feeling about it. "I think Valerie Young has a strong motive since she was Nadine's agent. It's been no secret that everyone who had come in direct contact with Nadine said that she was going to fire Valerie."

He was so good at listening this time without interrupting me. Or he just tuned me out. I was going with the idea he was listening, so I continued to tell him my theory and how Dawn had told me about the fifteen percent for life.

"It's true." I agreed one-hundred percent with the idea stars sometime become more popular in death. "Michael Jackson. Prince," I rattled off a couple of my all-time favorite stars. "Their album sales went through the roof. The same could be true for Nadine White. If Valerie knew Nadine was going to fire her, Valerie had to be thinking about her income. What better way to make it go up then rely on the fact that Nadine White's work would go up in value, making her income continue. Or at least giving her a jolt of income that could sustain her until she landed another big client."

"You make a very good point and I agree." Those words coming out of his mouth made my heart soar. We were connecting on so many levels that I truly believed my stars had aligned and my soul mate was actually right here in front of me. In Normal, Kentucky of all places. "If we could only find her."

"What?" I took my coat off once we were inside and took his from him, hanging them on the hook to dry.

He took off Fifi's leash and handed her a treat. She grabbed it and ran to her little bed near the front of the RV and began gnawing on it.

It was like Hank and I had a rhythm. He opened the Chinese bags and took out the containers while I grabbed a couple of plates.

"She came to the station to talk to me after she heard about Nadine." He put air quotes around heard as if he didn't believe her. He took a bottle of wine out of one of the bags and grabbed two coffee mugs since I didn't have wine glasses. He poured some in each and set them down on the table. "She said she was going to go back to the camper after we cleared it. I've called the phone number she gave me, and the phone has been disconnected. We've had a ranger camped out in the park behind the camper to watch for any movement."

"And?" I asked. We passed the containers between us, sharing them and putting some on our plates.

"She's not been back. Have you noticed anything?"

"No. I was waiting to go over and give my condolences while

figuring out how long she'd be staying, not to mention snoop a little." Now I wasn't going to wait to just let myself in and look around. "But I'm sure y'all combed the place."

"We took some fingerprints. That's about it. We found a few prints that weren't Abby's at the scene and I'm hoping to see if any of them match. We sent them off and should have those back in a day or so." He picked at the beef and broccoli with his fork until he found a bite.

"What about Reed Fowler?" I asked.

"What about him? We had him arrested." Hank didn't see it as big of a deal as me.

"When?" I asked.

"The day you saw me and Nadine at the diner. That was him taking photos of her." The images of his and Nadine's fingers touching played in my head as she handed him that paper, which I knew was now the restraining order. "That's when she told me about the restraining order she had against him. Apparently, if anyone got wind about what she was working on while she was here, there was a huge reward from one of those slimy magazines."

"Yeah. I knew that. But I think he might be a good suspect to look at too. Because he has the monetary motive like Valerie. Plus," I put my finger up when Hank went to say something, so I could finish my thought, "he had to be mad that she took out a restraining order against him and had him thrown in jail."

"I'd say he would be a good suspect, but he's still in jail. His hearing to post bond was postponed due to the judge not being able to get to the courthouse in this weather." Hank's words deflated me.

I sure thought my sleuthing skills were getting better and better.

"Okay, then. . ." I sighed deeply and reached over to the kitchen counter from my chair to grab the notebook. "I've got to cross him off my list."

That only left me with one person. Valerie Young.

Not only did she have the perfect motive, she'd disappeared. Looked guilty to me.

CHAPTER SIXTEEN

The next morning, I woke up with the early alarm to get ready for the early shift at the office since it was my turn to open. There was a text on my cell phone from Ava Grady.

Ava: All taken care for you. Got Abby in the right frame of mind. She remembered where and what happened. Obviously, didn't kill the author. You owe me $400. I dropped her off at your friend Queenie's house. You can find her there.

I gulped back the amount. It was worth it since she got Abby off. Instead of thinking anymore about paying Ava, I went ahead and Venmo'd the amount to her. It was a form of payment sort of like PayPal. I put the phone back on the nightside table.

"Are you ready to get up?" I put my hand on Fifi, who was sleeping on the pillow next to me. She was all curled up in a tight ball with her little eyes open. "I feel the same way." I pulled the quilt up to my chin. "Just a few more minutes."

A knock at the door ruined that thought. It made Fifi jump up with a yip or two.

"Do you think it's Hank?" The excitement of the possibility it was him made me jump out of bed and dart to the door. I picked up Fifi first. If I didn't do that, she'd dart out the door and that wasn't going to happen, especially since I didn't have on the right clothes to chase her in the snow.

"Hi. I'm Laura." The young woman I'd invited to come to the library to meet Nadine White was standing at my door. "I heard the news about Nadine White and I just had to come here. I went to the office, but the note said to come here." She shivered as she stood on the bottom step.

"Come in." I opened the door for her. Fifi shivered after she stuck her little black nose out the door. She ran back into the bedroom where I'm sure she was snuggled up again on the pillow. "I just got up, but I'll make us some coffee."

If I remembered correctly in my morning brain fog, Laura was drinking coffee at the diner when I'd met her.

"Thank you," she gratefully sighed. "I've not slept all night."

"I heard Nadine was going to mentor you." Valerie had mentioned that in hopes it'd make Nadine look a little nicer. I worked around the kitchen getting the coffee grounds in the maker and turning the button on for the coffee maker to brew. Within seconds, the RV smelled like the yummy aroma that started to wake up my senses.

"Yeah. I even dropped off my manuscript to her and I've been trying to get in touch with Valerie Young about it, but she won't call me back." Laura fumbled with the buttons on her wool coat. "I just went by the camper to stay there until she came out, but the car isn't there and she's not there either."

"Valerie hasn't been back in a day or so." I was really starting to think she was the one who did kill Nadine. "Did you hear Valerie and Nadine argue or fight when you dropped off your book?"

"No, but Nadine did tell me that she and Valerie were parting ways. She said that Valerie was so mad at her for it. They were going to meet for supper at that The Red Barn and discuss it before Nadine took some sort of I'm sorry package to Abby, which by the way," Laura lifted her hands to her chest, "I'm so happy to hear she's no longer a suspect. Abby is one of the reasons I love going to the library. I can sit in there for hours and she's so kind. She's always bringing me coffee."

"Speaking of coffee." I grabbed two mugs from the hooks off the wall where they hung and poured me and Laura a nice big cup. "Cheers."

"Here's to finding out who killed Nadine." Her voice trailed off with deep sadness. "Or at least finding Valerie so I can get my book back."

"No doubt. Is it the only copy you have?" I asked.

"Yes. I'm very old school. I even use a typewriter." She laughed with the mug up to her mouth. The steam of the hot coffee parted down the middle as her breath hit it. "I knew better than to give her the only copy, but it's Nadine White. She offered, and I jumped at it."

"At least you know she was interested." I shrugged thinking how awful Laura must've felt to get so close to a famous author looking at her work. "Plus, I'm sure it's hard to put all your heart into it and have someone critique it."

"Yes. That's the hardest part of trying to fulfill my passion to write. Getting thick enough skin to let someone tear it apart." She took a sip. "But, then it only makes you a better writer. If you're open to the criticism."

"That would be hard," I said and sipped more coffee.

We talked about her dreams and how she'd decided to become a writer. It was fascinating watching her talk. The passion she had for it poured out of her. She spoke about the written word and all the books that'd changed her life. It was nice to be reassured there were still passionate people in the world.

"You're going to make it. You are very determined." I couldn't help but notice her focus and drive.

"Thank you for the coffee." She pointed to my notebook on the counter. "Can I write my phone number in case Valerie comes back or you find my manuscript in the camper?"

"Yes. No problem." I opened the notebook to the back and ripped out a page for her to write down her number. "I'll talk to Detective

Sharp to see if it's okay that I go in there, even though they've cleared it."

I referred to Hank as the detective because it felt funny to even think along the lines of a boyfriend. Even at my age, was he a boyfriend? A companion? After last night and the few kisses, I'd like to think it was more than companionship. It was something that I needed to let unfold naturally and not push it. He was someone I really wanted to date and see where this thing would go, not run him off.

"That'd be great." She scribbled down her number and grabbed her coat.

Fifi ran down the hallway back into the room. She scratched on the door.

"I'll follow you out." I put my feet into my snow boots before wrapping up in my coat and snapping Fifi's leash on her collar. "Fifi needs to go out."

I couldn't help but look across the lake at the camper Nadine had rented. The outside Christmas lights were on, but the car wasn't there and the camper was completely dark. I found that most campers who rented from me always kept a light on. They felt safer, at least that's what they'd said.

Fifi didn't take long to do her business. Within a half hour of Laura leaving, I'd gotten my shower and was dressed for the day. It was going to be cold and I knew I wanted to check out Reed on Facebook and see how I could find him. He and Valerie were two people I still believed had great motive to kill Nadine.

Nadine had a restraining order against Reed. She was a big pay day to anyone who could reveal what she was working on. If they only knew it was a cookbook. Then there was Valerie. She had the biggest motive between the two. Her entire income was based on her being Nadine's agent. If Nadine didn't keep her as her agent, Valerie's income would drop, though she'd still have a steady flow from the past book deals she'd made for Nadine. Plus the assumption of Nadine's worth going up after death, like Dawn had suggested, was a real thing. At least, real enough to have killed her for it.

I flipped open the notebook where I'd written all of it down. Everything Laura had told me about Nadine's thoughts on Valerie were spot on with why now I knew it was more important than ever to find Valerie Young.

CHAPTER SEVENTEEN

I was happy to see the snow had really stopped. Not that I didn't love it, but I was looking forward to spending the time with old and new friends at the monthly themed party Christmas Dinner at the Campground on Christmas Day, which was just a few days away.

It would be a much-needed break from all the hullabaloo of the murder. Hopefully, Hank would get the word out nationally that they were on the lookout for Valerie Young. Last night before he left, he did say they'd called in the FBI to get her on the most wanted list, which meant that any sleuthing from this point on was just merely for my curious side.

Which was in full bloom, since I found myself going over to the camper Nadine had rented after I'd gone to the office, checked the voicemails, and answered a few emails while I waited for more coffee to brew to keep me warm on my walk down there.

The camper was one of the cutest little things I'd ever seen, and I hoped Nadine had found some joy in staying there while she was here. She certainly wasn't messy. Her suitcase was still on the bed with it open. I looked through it and noticed she'd brought items that were comfy like leggings, a few big sweaters, and some fuzzy socks. It looked like a writer ready to hunker down outfit to me. If there were such a thing.

The items in the bathroom were what I'd expected to see from a famous person. Only the best haircare products and perfumes that I'd gotten accustomed to when I was married to Paul West. Those items were long in my past and the Dollar Tree was my cosmetics counter since I had a limited income. Even seeing Nadine's things didn't tug at my heartstrings or make me long for those items. It was just stuff. What I felt inside and had gained from Normal was a true family, friends, community, and a sense of belonging.

All of this nostalgia made me think of Mary Elizabeth. At some point, I was going to have to live up to my promise and sit down with her to discuss whatever it was she wanted to discuss about our relationship.

After going through the camper one more time, I figured no one was going to come back. As I began to pick up the items to take up to the office, I looked under things to try to find Laura's manuscript. Wouldn't that be a great Christmas gift I could give her.

"Yoo-hoo!" Mary Elizabeth's voice called out from the front of the camper. "I seen you come in here, May-bell-ine."

I truly wished she'd just call me Mae.

"Back here," I called back and swallowed my emotions. "Why don't you come back here and help me get Nadine's things together for Dawn."

I didn't have to repeat myself. She was back there before I could pick up anything else to put in the suitcase.

"How did the date go?" She smiled with a twinkle in her eye. "Darlin', he's cuter than a litter of puppies," she gushed.

I couldn't help but smile. Mary Elizabeth always had a way with words and with how she saw the world. When I was living with her, it just got on my nerves. Now I actually liked hearing them again. That's why I decided to tell her about the date and how we'd made snow angels.

"I know it seems so childish, but Paul was so much older than me when we briefly dated." I put the makeup items in Nadine's bag. "I wasn't truly enjoying just living. Paul threw me into the social scene and all the fine things that money could buy."

As I talked about my life with Paul and how I'd finally realized money wasn't what was important to me anymore, the more I saw she was truly listening. Not interrupting or even giving her advice. She was actually not butting in but listening to what I was saying.

"I guess I better stop rambling and get back to the office." I closed the suitcase and looked at Mary Elizabeth. Her silence was deafening. There were some tears rolling down her face. "Are you okay?"

"This." She held her hands open towards me. "You. You have turned out to be a joy. I know it was hard for you to come live with me. You had your own mama, but I felt so sorry for you. I wanted to try to give you a different life than you knew before so the pain you were feeling from your old life was not at bad."

It was my turn to truly listen to her. I'd never let her do that. I sat on the edge of the bed in front of her and let her talk.

"I love your curls." She reached out and touched my hair. "I wanted you to be so happy and I knew those little rich girls could be so mean. I only wanted you to fit in and have a life where no one felt sorry for you because you were orphaned. I wanted them to see the true beautiful you and for you not hide behind your curls. That's why I got your hair straightened. That's why I made you take so many classes." She wiped the tears from her face. "I see now that you found your way. Without me, you found your way."

She sat down next to me. There we were sitting on a camper bed next to each other in silence. An act so simple, though we found it so hard to do years ago without fighting one another, when we truly wanted best for each other.

"Mary Elizabeth, I'm so grateful you gave me a home. It wasn't your job to fix me. I was and will always be so sad about my family. But I wasn't mature enough to see the life that you were trying to give me. I was a teenager that thought you were trying to take my mom's place. Trying to undo everything they'd ever taught me." I pointed to my chest. "But I know that she gave me the best of her and you gave me the best of you, making me who I am in here."

"I do love you, Mae," she said the words I longed to hear for the ten years I'd been gone.

"I love you too," I gulped back my pride, "Mom."

Her tears turned to sobs as she grabbed me in one of her big southern mama hugs that she tried to give me when I was younger. It felt right giving her the title she had tried so hard to get. For the first time, I truly felt like my own mom would want me to give Mary Elizabeth that title from her as her gift from heaven.

There were no other words said between us as we sat on that bed for what seemed like hours but was only a few minutes.

"Now, we got that out of the way." She stood up and brushed off her sweater like she was just sweeping it all away. It was her way of brushing it under the rug and moving on. This conversation would never be spoken of again, we both knew that. "We need to head to the office with this stuff and work on our investigation."

"About that. . ." I showed her out of the camper and sent a quick text to Henry that he could clean the camper and get it ready for the next renter.

On our trek through the snow on our way back to the office, I told her about Reed being in jail for breaking the restraining order and how Valerie had skipped town, making the FBI's list of most wanted for the murder of Nadine White. I also told her about Laura's manuscript and how I'd been trying to find it in the camper.

Mary Elizabeth poured herself a cup of coffee and refilled my cup once we were back in the office, out of the cold.

"I bet Valerie has it and is going to publish it herself." Mary Elizabeth made a light bulb go off in my head.

"What did you say?" I asked. A text chirped from my pocket.

"I said that Valerie probably took it and will publish it for herself."

"You!" I jumped for joy.

"What? That screamin' of yours would scare the beard off Jesus!" She looked shocked.

"I think you just solved the last piece of the puzzle." I couldn't be any happier in this moment.

"Me?" She drew back.

"What if Valerie Young was Nadine White's ghost writer?" When the words came out of my mouth, I knew I was right. I grabbed Nadine's renter file and my purse. "I need you to watch the office while I go somewhere."

CHAPTER EIGHTEEN

I tried calling Hank on my way to the Bluegrass Airport in Lexington since I knew I couldn't text him while I was driving. I had to tell him that I remembered Valerie mentioning something about a meeting with the publisher in a couple of days. That meant it was today. It also reminded me how much Valerie was trying to change Nadine's mind about the cookbook concept and was trying to get her to do another romance with the ghost writer. She was so determined that I just knew that Valerie was the ghost writer. And that was why Nadine had to get rid of her.

Not the fact she was the agent, she was the writer and Nadine was not going to have her name on those books anymore. She wanted a clean break and the only way out was doing what was in her heart. A cookbook.

It all made sense in my head and when I started to fumble my words on Hank's answering machine, I just gave up.

"Forget it. Call me. I'm driving to Lexington to see if I'm right and the meeting is happening." I threw the phone down in the seat and drove the curvy roads.

I was happy to see the county road was cleared and that I even passed a few salt trucks with plows. County roads were the first ones maintained during snow emergencies. Sometimes it took forever to get somewhere when one of the salt trucks got in front of you, but today I was grateful for the clear path that was leading me exactly where I needed to be.

I parked in short-term parking and hurried inside. I knew if Valerie and the publisher were meeting, they had to meet outside of the secured part since Valerie didn't have a plane ticket to get inside the security, unless she'd recently bought one. I let all those things float out of my mind because I trusted that Hank had done his job and put traces on the rental car and flagged Valerie's name, alerting him or the FBI if she'd tried to get a plane ticket. At least, that's what the sleuths on TV did. From my experience, they weren't too terribly different.

As if divine intervention had crossed my path, in the distance on a couch near the baggage claim sat Valerie Young and a man in a suit.

"Valerie," I had walked up behind her. She turned her head and then adjusted her body to turn slightly behind herself.

"Mae." Nervously, she looked between me and the man. "Dan, this is Mae West. A friend of mine." Her words were so convincing, for a second, I thought I was wrong. "Mae, this is Dan. He's Nadine's editor. We were just discussing how we are going to approach Nadine's last book she was working on."

The man stood up and shook my hand. His grip was so hard, it nearly took me to my knees. He gave me a good hard stare that frightened me.

"Can I talk to you for a minute?" I jerked my hand back before he stopped the blood flow and my hand fell off my arm.

Valerie gave Dan her polite smile and excused herself. The horn above the carousel in the baggage claim sounded and the belt started to move, sending luggage from a flight down and around, making a screeching noise.

"Why did you kill her? Are you her ghost writer?" I asked, though the sound was so loud I had to be louder.

"Keep your voice down." She glared at me. Her jaw tensed. "I had to do what I had to do."

"You are a murderer and I'm calling Hank to let him know I found you." I reached around my pocket for my phone and realized I'd thrown it on the seat in my car after I'd left Hank a message.

Valerie reached out and grabbed me by my arm, digging her nails into me. I winced from the pain.

"You're not going to call anyone. You are going to go over there with me and get this deal done so I can have one last book published. Then, if you are a good girl, I might just be kind and kill you fast. If you aren't the good girl like your foster mom wishes you were, then your death will be slow and painful." Her words sent chills all over me. She didn't leave any room for negotiation for my life. Either way she was going to kill me.

I did what she said and walked back over to Dan with her death grip now on the flappy part of my upper arm. She pinched it so hard, I was in pain. While she made her deal with Dan, it would give me time to figure out what I needed to do to alert the security officer just feet away from me that I was taken hostage by a crazy lady. My heart was beating. My palms were sweating. My mouth was dry. It seemed like we were sitting there forever, and my brain had gone to mush. I couldn't think past beyond the pain of her stepping on my toe.

"That settles it." She had the toe of her shoe on my boot, pressing down, letting me know that she was well aware I was still there and that we had a deal. "I'll write the next book with the sweet town setting and all the family and relationships as Nadine White's last novel. I'm glad we agreed to a final settlement of a one million dollars advance." She had the contract they'd just negotiated in her hands.

"Not before we write up the ending." Hank Sharp had walked up behind the couch and put a heavy hand on Valerie Young's shoulder, causing her to wince out in pain. "Thank you, Dan."

I jumped to my feet. Dan opened his shirt to show where there was a wire taped to him.

"I thought you were going to blow my cover," Dan gasped for air. "I was dying sitting there. Valerie Young can be a mean person."

"Are you really the editor?" I was so confused by what was going on.

"Yes. The FBI contacted the publishing house and we sent over all the contracts. Valerie Young was a ghost writer for her and that's when they told me to keep this meeting. They didn't give me a choice not to be wired up." Dan finished off telling me about Nadine and how she'd come to the publishing house.

Dan told us that Valerie had once been a great writer, but turned crazy after they broke her publishing contract and became an agent. She saw Nadine as fresh talent and knew she could enhance it. That's when Nadine talked Valerie into co-writing using her as a ghost writer. All these years Nadine had felt stuck in a writing relationship she didn't find true to her heart.

"That was close." I was so happy to have Hank walk me back to my car.

"When I saw you walk into the airport, my heart sank. I wasn't about to let anything happen to you now that I found you." Hank brushed my curls out of my face. His hand rested on my cheek. "It was then that I realized that you stole my heart the first time I saw you with the lake scum all in your hair."

"That awful day." I had just moved to the campground and the lake was nasty. I was standing on the rickety pier with Henry trying to figure out what I needed to do to get the lake looking good so I could sell the darn campground. The pier gave way and both of us fell into the lake just as Hank and his then partner were driving up to question me about Paul's escape from jail. I had nasty moss and scum stuck in my hair and I was drenched from head to toe.

"You were so natural in that moment. So vulnerable even though you gave me heck and hated the campground." He moved his other hand to the other side of my cheek, cradling my face. "Don't scare me like this again."

"I called to tell you where I was going." I stared into his big green eyes and could feel my heart warm.

"If you don't hear from me, don't do it." He warned me, sealing it with a kiss.

"You mean, you're going to keep using me in your investigations?" I smiled.

CHAPTER NINETEEN

I flipped on the radio station on my way back to Normal. Christmas tunes were playing, and I was singing along to Here Comes Santa Claus just as the snow started to tumble out of the sky. It was going to be a wonderful Christmas now that Nadine White's killer had been taken into custody.

I'd checked my phone messages before I'd hit the road. The text that'd come through earlier that I didn't read was from Christine at the Cookie Crumble Bakery. She said she was ready to start on the candy cane donuts for the Christmas Dinner at the Campground that was in a couple of days.

Today Dottie had planned to get all the decorations and paperware for the dinner before she had to come to work. With Mary Elizabeth at the office, I gave her a quick call to make sure she was okay and to let her know that I was going to run by the Milkery to get the ingredients Christine needed before I came back to finish my day at the office. I also gave her a brief rundown of what had happened at the airport.

I knew by the time I ran my errand, news about what had taken place at the airport would be all over Normal and I'd be fielding calls left and right.

Since the snow plows had put down salt, the big falling flakes were melting on impact, making it the perfect time for me to visit the Milkery. There were large silos around the property with the dairy's name printed on each of them. The cows were all huddled together on one side of the Kentucky post fence up the drive and the other side looked to be enclosed chicken houses where the free-range chickens lived.

"What on earth are you doing out here?" I heard someone call out to me when I got out of my car.

"Laura," I was happy to see her. "What are you doing here?"

"I live here." She held a metal pail with chicken eggs stacked to the top. "My aunt and uncle own the farm and I work it."

"That's so cool. I've never been here." I looked around and tried to picture just how colorful it was during the warmer months. Currently, the trees that surrounded the farm were bare and the white snow covered everything. "I'm here to get some ingredients for Christine over at the Cookie Crumble Bakery to make her candy cane donuts for my Christmas Dinner at the Campground." I smiled. "Say, you and your aunt and uncle should come."

"I'll see. They take Christmas around here pretty seriously." She nodded towards the farm house sitting off into the distance. "Come on, I'll show you around." She set the basket of eggs on the picnic table along the way. "Christine called and said someone would be by to get enough ingredients for over one-hundred donuts, but she didn't say it was you. Those eggs are part of your order."

"Wow. It fascinates me how this place works and how our community really supports each other." It was such a great feeling to have at this time of the year and it really enhanced the season of giving.

"I'm pretty fortunate that my aunt and uncle really believe in my writing. You know it's hard to be a writer." She didn't tell me anything I hadn't figured out over the past few days.

"Speaking of writers." I had to tell her about Valerie. "They've Valerie in custody for killing Nadine."

"Really?" She asked with big eyes right before we took off our boots to head into the farm house. "What happened?"

I told her all about how Mary Elizabeth had given me the idea that

Valerie was the ghost writer and how I vaguely remembered her saying the publisher or someone from the publishing house was going to be meeting them at the airport.

"He was wired? She confessed?" Laura seemed to be a little stunned. "That's so wild."

We had some chit-chat about the process Valerie would go through with murder charges while she showed me the house and her typewriter where she did her work.

"I did break down and ask for a laptop for Christmas to write on." She'd finally given in to technology.

"Good for you." I looked around the office. The view from the window was amazing. Off in the distance were the mountains of the Daniel Boone National Park. Somewhere in there was Happy Trails Campground. "This is really an inspiring view to write to," I said louder than normal after Laura had excused herself to go to the bathroom.

I leaned on the desk to see what was below the window and my foot knocked over a trash can full of papers.

I bent down to pick them up and noticed the red ink all over them.

"There is way too much dialog in this. You'll never get to be a writer if you don't start adding descriptions," I read out loud.

I put that paper down and picked up a fistful. All of them had red writing on them and nothing good to say. Each comment was worse than the other. The last page I picked up had a longer paragraph.

"You cannot be a writer at this time. I will not be able to mentor you until you get some writing classes under your belt. You are going to waste your time and mine until you figure out the structure of sentences and the proper usage of verbs, pronouns, and emotions. Your characters have the emotions of a white Saltine cracker. And you didn't bring me along with the plot. Each chapter has to have something to do with the romance. Your lovers go for pages without a kiss. Good luck, you're going to need it. Nadine," my voiced trailed. I blinked several times to make sure I was actually seeing what I was seeing.

"What did you say?" Laura came back into the room. Her eyes focused on my hands where I was holding the manuscript she told me that Nadine had and she hadn't gotten back. "You weren't supposed to find that."

"I thought you said. . ." Images of the eggs, donuts, the thought of poison appeared in my head. "You have access to the ingredients."

"Oh, now you're going to figure it out?" She let out a spurt of evil laughs. "I really should've tried my hand at crime fiction, because in real life, I've definitely pulled it off."

"You?" I asked confused as to why.

"Yeah, me. I don't know how I lucked out with Valerie showing up and stabbing Nadine in the neck after she was already dead from the poison I had put in her special milk she had asked for to bake with." She unhooked the belt from around her waistband and snapped the straps together, making me jump. "It was perfect, really. Nadine whatever her name is deserved to die. She was so jealous of my talent that she wrote those terrible words, so I wouldn't take away her readers."

Now I knew Laura was delusional and it looked like she would have no problem killing me with that belt. I put my hands up to my neck as she walked closer and closer to me.

"She gave me the manuscript with all the writing on it. She knew I couldn't send it off to publishers like that. I am going to have to retype it all, but without her around, it just makes the door wide open for me to claim my destiny." She inhaled with a big smile on her face. A look of satisfaction in her eyes. "She gave it to me that afternoon then asked me if I could supply her with the special milk. Oh yeah. I did. I even delivered the milk to her at the Normal Diner and waited. I didn't realize she was going to go to the library, but it was perfect because I followed her there and when she was in the office I watched as the poison took her last breath. It was so satisfying."

She stopped when she got a foot closer to me.

"Do you want me to tell you how she convulsed, falling into the chair, and I stood over her spouting off her lies about my book?" She grinned, bringing the belt level with my neck. "I'd been there a little, while making sure I would see her take her last breath. Then, I heard the front doors of the library open and hid behind the office desk.

"Nadine's back was to the door as she sat there dead in the chair. I heard Valerie call her name and before I knew it, Nadine's body had dropped to the ground. Her face pointed at me while her eyes were open with a knife sticking straight out of her neck."

As the faint sounds of sirens swirled in the air outside, my head told me help was on the way, letting me take a few deep breaths to regain my senses. When Laura turned her head toward the sirens, I jumped on her, tackling her to the ground.

She grabbed a fistful of my hair, sending my head back. She karate chopped my neck, making me gag and stumble to my knees. She lunged, wrapping her fingers around my neck and squeezing as tight as she could.

There was pressure on my esophagus. My lungs gasped for air, but a raspy wheeze escaped me. I tugged on both of her wrists to try to pry her hands off of me. Her mouth was open. Her teeth were clenched. Her eyes looked dead. She was a killer.

"Let her go!" Hank yelled. My eyes caught sight of him standing behind her with his gun pointed at her.

"Shooooooot," I tried to say in a last-ditch effort to save myself.

A shot rang out. Ringing in my ears forced my eyes closed. Laura's hands fell away from my neck as she fell to the ground, grasping her leg. Before I could even recover a full breath, Hank had her on the ground with her hands cuffed behind her back.

CHAPTER TWENTY

"Merry Christmas!" Mary Elizabeth entered the recreation center in her full-length fur coat and matching hat. Her hands were full of presents.

"Merry Christmas," I hurried over and greeted her, Bobby Ray right behind me. He grabbed the presents and I grabbed her, giving her a big southern hug. "Merry Christmas."

"Merry Christmas." Hank Sharp came over and hugged her too. He looked so handsome in the ugly Christmas sweater that was on the flyer put up around town.

"My goodness." Mary Elizabeth pulled back. Her eyes drew up and down his body. "Even in that ugly sweater, you're finer than a frog hair split six ways." She licked her lips.

"Stop it right now." I rolled my eyes. "You're early. We are getting all the tablecloths on the tables and the food will be delivered any minute.

"I brought a friend." As she said that, Dawn Gentry walked in. Of course her Christmas sweater had a Santa in a biker outfit on it. "I've got news. We've got news." Mary Elizabeth nudged Dawn. "Tell her."

"As you know, Kelli Sergeant and her husband put the Milkery Dairy Farm up for sale since they think their niece has ruined them." She smiled so big that I already knew what was coming. "Since I'm a chef and Mary Elizabeth is looking to move closer to her children..." obviously she was referring to me and Bobby Ray.

"We've decided to buy it and partner up!" Mary Elizabeth was worse than Bobby Ray. She couldn't wait for Dawn to tell it and he couldn't wait to open his presents.

He was already through three of the ones Mary Elizabeth had brought him.

"Really?" I bounced with excitement. "That's wonderful news!"

I never in a million years thought I would say that I was happy to be living near my foster mother again. Especially after her no-nonsense talk had led me to pin the murder on Valerie. According to the final autopsy report, and what clued Hank in, was the timing of the stab wound and how the poisonous mushroom Boletus had been found in her system. It just so happened that Ty and Dawn didn't try the recipe that called for special milk. That's how they weren't poisoned. When Hank interviewed Dawn, she told him about the local writer who had dropped off the milk, but it didn't click until he'd gotten a call from Colonel Holz while taking Valerie Young back to the station.

It was Valerie who told him Laura's name. He put two and two together. That type of mushroom was found in the Daniel Boone National Park, which lead him to believe it was Laura who had poisoned the milk she gave to Nadine out of anger over the bad review Dawn said Nadine had told her about.

When he called me at the office and Mary Elizabeth told him I was running out to the Milkery to pick up the ingredients for the candy cane donuts, he knew he had little time to get out there before I put two and two together.

"Hey, are you okay?" Hank walked up behind me and wrapped his arms around me, resting his chin on my shoulder.

"I'm more than okay." I twisted around. Despite the noise from the caterers setting up the Christmas dinner that'd come from Normal Diner and from Christine setting up the dessert station, I got lost in Hank's eyes. "I'm happier than I ever thought I could be."

I took his hand in mine and turned back around. Everything and everyone that I loved was in this room. It was one of the best Christmases I'd had in a long time.

Dottie was holding Fifi as she, Queenie, Betts, and Abby were huddled in a corner. Ty and Abby had made up. There definitely wasn't any chemistry between him and Dawn that I could see.

Then it happened. The Laundry Club circle opened just as I let go of Hank's hand and joined my friends. Only I wasn't the only stranger they let into their group. Dawn Gentry was the newest member of the Laundry Club.

The End

Want more of Mae West and the Laundry Club Ladies?
The next book in the series, MOTORHOMES, MAPS, & MURDER, is now available to purchase or read in Kindle Unlimited. And read on for a sneak peek.

But wait! Readers ask me how much my cozy mysteries and the characters in them reflect my real life. Well…here is a good story for you.

Whooo hooo!! I'm so glad we are a week out from last Coffee Chat with Tonya and happy to report the poison ivy is almost gone! But y'all we got more issues than Time magazine up in our family.
When y'all ask me if my real life ever creeps into books, well…grab your coffee because here is a prime example!
My sweet mom's birthday was over the weekend. Now, I'd already decided me and Rowena was going to stay there for a couple of extra days.
On her birthday, Sunday, Tracy and David were there too, and we were talking about what else…poison ivy! I was telling them how I can't stand not shaving my legs. Mom and Tracy told me they don't shave daily and I might've curled my nose a smidgen. And apparently it didn't go unnoticed.
I went inside the house to start cooking breakfast for everyone and mom went up to her room to get her bathing suit on and Tracy was with me. All the men were already outside on the porch.
The awfulest crash came from upstairs and my sister tore out of that kitchen like a bat out of hell and I kept flipping the bacon. My mom had fallen…shaving her legs!
Great. Now it's my fault.
Her wrist was a little stiff but she kept saying she was fine. We had a great day. We celebrated her birthday, swam, and had cake. When it came time for everyone to leave but me and Ro, I told mom that she should probably go get an x-ray because her wrist was a little swollen. After a lot of coaxing, she agreed and I put my shoes on and told Tracy, David, and Eddy to go on home and we'd call them.
My mama looked me square in the face and said, "You're going with that top knot on your head?"
I said, "yes."
She sat back down in the chair and said, "I'm not going with you lookin' like that."

"Are you serious?" I asked.

"Yes. I'm dead serious. I'm not going with you looking like that. What if we see someone?" She was serious, y'all!

She protested against my hair!

Now...this is exactly like the southern mama's I write about! I looked at Eddy and he was laughing. Tracy and David were laughing and I said, "I can't wait until I tell my coffee chat people about this."

As you can see in the above photo, the before and after photo.

Yep...we went and she broke her wrist! Can you believe that? We were a tad bit shocked, and I'll probably be staying a few extra days (which will give us even more to talk about over coffee next week).

Oh...we didn't see anyone we knew so I could've worn my top knot! As I'm writing this, you can bet your bottom dollar my hair is pulled up in my top knot!

Okay, so y'all might be asking why I'm putting this little story in the back of my book, well, that's a darn tootin' good question.

This is exactly what you can expect when you sign up for my newsletter. There's always something going on in my life that I have to chat with y'all about each Tuesday on Coffee Chat with Tonya. Go to Tonyakappes.com and click on subscribe in the upper right corner to join.

Chapter One of Book Five
Motorhomes, Maps, & Murder

"Why didn't they teach us about this in school?" I asked Queenie French, who was standing over the conference table in the Normal Public Library, about the history of the Battle of Camp Wildcat.

She didn't stop looking over the map of the Daniel Boone National Park where the Battle of Camp Wildcat had taken place during the Civil War.

"They oughta since it happened right here in our state." She shook her head and a strand of short blonde hair escaped from a bobby pin. She pointed to Sheltowee Trace National Recreation Trail near the Happy Trails Campground, the campground I owned and called home.

"That there trail played a big part." She pulled the bobby pin from her hair and pried it apart with her teeth and fingertips before she snugged the wayward hair to her head. "Colonel Theophilus T. Garrard stood right there commanding the thousands of men in his troop." She reached down and unzipped her fanny pack, taking out a few more bobby pins and sticking them all over her head.

"You put on this reenactment every year during the spring?" I questioned the accuracy of the event since the real battle took place the morning of October 21, 1861.

At least that's what I'd read in the Normal Gazette, the local newspaper, in the section where they'd been featuring the reenactment to help spread the word.

"Mmmhmm," her lips pressed together as she stood up straight, pushing the orange headband up on her forehead a little more. "During the spring was when they got word of the invasion. It took all summer to gather the troops and get them in position. Our first few reenactments were in October on the actual battle day, but the weather gets so wonky here that every year it was either raining or snowing, making it hard for everyone to sit outside all day." She laughed. "You should've seen old Henry the last year we had it in October." She was talking about my handyman at Happy Trails. "It was cold as all get out. He nearly froze to a popsicle while he laid there the four hours. He was the first one dead."

"What?" I'd never been to a reenactment, much less participated in one. All of this seemed really fascinating to me.

"What do you mean, what?" Her eyes lowered, giving me the look. "You mean to tell me you ain't ever seen a reenactment before?"

"I have in the movie Sweet Home Alabama with Reece Witherspoon," I shrugged and tucked a piece of my long curly hair behind my ear.

"You're in for a treat." A young woman I recognized as the cashier from Tough Nickel Thrift Shop strolled into the conference room. She had a map in her hands and laid it on top of the one I was looking at.

"Then you seen enough of a reenactment to know that the people from both sides who are shot have to lay there until the battle is over. It's a real reenactment with guns and everything, Mae." She said my name like I should've known better.

"This is why I said it should've been taught in school," I said, turning my attention back to the script that Queenie had given to all the actors. I used the term actor very loosely, meaning me. "I figured you'd been gone from Kentucky too long to play a good role like a nurse, so I have you watering the horses for the soldiers near their camp site." She handed me an apron that'd seen better days. "You'll put this overtop your uniform."

"Reporting that there's no signs of typhoid fever, smallpox, measles, diarrhea, pneumonia, or malaria," said the young woman as she saluted Queenie.

Queenie beamed.

"You're the best nurse in the war," Queenie said as the two embraced.

"I'm Mae West." I properly introduced myself. "I've seen you at the Tough Nickel Thrift Store."

"Yes. I have seen you come in a time or two." She smiled at me, waves of short, light brown hair framing her face. She had side swept bangs that showed off her pretty blue eyes. "I'm Julip Kaye Knox."

"She's not just a clerk at the thrift store, she's on the board of the Historical Society. She knows the ins and outs of every map," Queenie bragged. She definitely liked Julip. "I couldn't put on this reenactment without her knowledge of the layout of this battle."

"You would've done just fine." Julip patted Queenie on the back. "Excuse me while I go grab some more maps."

Queenie wasted no time getting back to my duties as horse wrangler.

"Here." Queenie picked up a large sealed plastic bag and shoved it against my chest. "It's your outfit. In addition to the apron." She motioned to my shoulder where I'd flung the apron. "Now, don't you lose any part of it. These are real, true to life uniforms. Replicas really. But you'll find the real ones in the Daniel Boone National Park museum located in their offices."

"I'll be sure to check that out." I took the bag from my chest and held up it in the air when I noticed Hank Sharp beyond the hangers. He strolled into the room like he owned it.

Our eyes met. He smiled and it traveled all the way up his green eyes.

"Good afternoon," he said and bent down to give me a kiss.

"Hi." I crinkled my nose and lifted my hand up to rub over his black hair. "It looks like you got a haircut for your part."

"Queenie insisted I had to if I was going to be a soldier." He pulled away from me, straightened his body, clicked his heels, and saluted Queenie.

"Now if you two think that y'all are going to play kissy face during the reenactment, you're wrong. You're on opposite sides of the battle." She wiggled her finger between us. "But I do like seeing the two of you happy."

"I like making her happy." Hank winked.

"It's not hard to do." I felt like a giddy teenager.

It was a very new relationship, me and Hank. Just a few months. We didn't see each other every day, but usually did most days. And when we did, it was at my RV at Happy Trails. I'd yet to see his place, although I knew from his granny, Agnes Swift, that he lived on his parents' property in a trailer on the south side of town, even though his parents had retired and moved to Florida.

"Geez," Queenie rolled her eyes and shook her head. "I'll be right back. I have to go get your bayonet and uniform. Not everyone can handle a bayonet." She wagged her finger over her shoulder at Hank on her way out of the conference room.

I'd been in Normal for about ten months and never thought I'd find love, especially at a campground in Kentucky.

Not that I didn't love the campground. I had grown to love it. I'd grown up in Kentucky, but as soon as the clock struck midnight on my eighteenth birthday, I was on a Greyhound bus to New York City where I worked my way through flight attendant school.

That's when my life took a turn that changed everything. I'd met an older, wealthy, investment man on one of my flights, who hired me as his personal flight attendant. We fell in love, got married, and lived a life of luxury that always seemed too good to be true. Turned out it was.

Like Queenie always says, if it seems too good to be true, it is.

If only I'd known her back then. After a few years of marriage, Paul West had taken all his clients, including several in Normal, to the cleaners. This put him in jail and uprooted me from my life of luxury and into a rundown campground that he'd put in my name, which is why Happy Trails was the only thing the government didn't seize.

"Are you going over your lines?" Hank rubbed his hand down my back and looked down at the script in my hand.

"You mean my one line," I looked at the paper and continued, "Look, the troops are coming."

"You better put a little more oomph into it or Queenie will be mad." His southern drawl was like music to my ears and sent my heart soaring.

In the back of my head, I knew it was the honeymoon stage, but I was willing to see it through.

"Detective Sharp," he answered his ringing cell phone in his professional cop voice. "Mmmhmm," he hummed and stepped away from me for some privacy.

"He's gonna look so good in this," Queenie said as she walked back into the conference room and put her finger up to her mouth when she noticed Hank was on the phone. "Won't he?" she whispered and pulled up the plastic over the old uniform so I could see it better.

"He will." I laughed at the thought of seeing him in the old civil war uniform, pretending to stab and shoot someone with the bayonet. "That thing looks sharp."

"Oh, it is. I only let special people have one of these. It could poke someone's eye out." She gave a good hard nod. "I let him and Preacher Hager use them."

Preacher Hager was married to one of my and Queenie's best friends, Betts Hager.

"If you can't trust a cop and preacher, who can you trust?" I joked.

"Listen, I've got to go." Hank had walked back over to us. His face was stern, and his soft green eyes had turned back into stone like they did when he was on a case. He kissed my forehead while putting his phone back in the pocket of his black suit pants. "I'll call you later."

"What about the uniform?" Queenie called after him before he hurried out the door.

"I'll get it before the reenactment," he assured her as he called over his shoulder.

"I guess I can give it to you." She held the uniform bag in one hand and the bayonet in the other.

"No, thank you." If she thought I was going to be responsible for his uniform and bayonet and get in trouble if something happened to it, she had another thing coming. "I'll have enough of a hard time keeping up with mine."

"Mae West," she tsked. "Don't you be going and making me regret putting you in the reenactment. There's been citizens who grew up here that've applied for parts and I didn't let them participate." She looked at me from underneath her brows. "You get what I'm saying?"

"I'm honored." I wasn't about to let the sixty year old widow down - she'd seen enough trouble in her life. "But I don't want that thing in my possession." I pointed to the bayonet.

The doors of the conference room opened, and all the reenactment actors filed in, ready to get all of their equipment for tomorrow morning's big performance.

"One line!" Queenie used her hands to gesture like there was an airplane runway in front of her. "Give me your name and I'll check it off."

Julip came back in with a bunch of maps. Queenie ended up having me check off each person's name on the list as she handed them their uniform and Julip gave them a map and a script.

During my ten months in Normal, I'd made it my mission to undo all the wrong Paul West had done now that he couldn't do it since he'd been murdered. Another story for another time. But it felt good that I could stand here and help hand out the important uniforms that this community was built upon.

"Did you see Lester Hager come in here?" Queenie bit her lip and looked back towards the door after the last actor has left. There was one outfit with a bayonet left, and Preacher Hager's name was the only one not marked off the list.

"I didn't." Julip shrugged.

"I didn't see him either. Or Betts." My brows furrowed, realizing it was odd that Betts hadn't shown up, even though she didn't have a part. She usually attended all community events, being a successful businesswoman and the preacher's wife and all.

"I parked by the Laundry Club if you'd like me to take it to Betts," I suggested since I'd figured Betts was there doing the books for the laundromat since it was close to tax season, something she'd been complaining about.

"She's not there." Abby Fawn, the librarian, was picking up little Styrofoam cups and stray napkins from around the room. "She called. She and Lester have all them bible-thumping women from the church at the jail, trying to get them prisoners some religion." She threw the trash away and walked over to get the sealed plastic bag and bayonet.

"Alrighty. I guess I'll give it to him in the morning at the reenactment. Something that I never do, but since it's Lester, I'll make an exception." Queenie hung the uniform on the back of one the of the conference chairs and leaned the bayonet up against the table.

She removed all the bobby pins from around her head and ran her fingers through her short hair, fluffing up the top. She put the bobby pins in her fanny pack and adjusted it around her waist while she glanced over the list of actors.

"I think the reenactment committee did a real good job of coordinating everything. This went much smoother than last year," Julip mentioned while Abby nodded in agreement. "I'm sure everything will go perfectly tomorrow."

Abby took her phone out and started typing away. She was so good at social media and used that phone to spread the word about everything going on in Normal.

"I hear we're expecting a few thousand people. The biggest turnout we've ever had." Queenie nudged me. "This is why we have it during the spring. It honors the time and commitment both sides put into the battle. Plus, the weather is nice, which means a great turnout and more donations to the Camp Wildcat Preservation Foundation, who can use the money to teach more youth about our great state.

"Hashtag great state, hashtag Kentucky, hashtag Camp Wildcat reenactment, hashtag tomorrow, hashtag nine a.m.," Abby talked out loud as she typed her latest tweet to attract more tourists to our little hiking tow. "Need a place to stay in hashtag Normal? Hashtag Happy Trails Campground."

"Thanks for the shout out," I said to Abby.

Abby had been instrumental in my decision to stay and get the campground back up and running. Between my ability to talk with people and invest in our community and Abby's great marketing and social media skills, Normal's economy was thriving.

Minus the hiccups of a few murders, but that was all behind us now.

I was just hoping and praying that everything went as smoothly tomorrow at the reenactment as Queenie expected. If history repeated itself like it had over the last few months, there was going to be a hiccup.

MOTORHOMES, MAPS, & MURDER is now available and on
KINDLE UNLIMITED.

RECIPES AND CLEANING HACKS FROM MAE WEST AND THE LAUNDRY CLUB LADIES AT THE HAPPY TRAILS CAMPGROUND IN NORMAL KENTUCKY.

RV Hack #1

Some campers don't like to put holes on the walls inside of their RV and campers, but we love the luxury of having curtains hanging on the windows to offer that at home feel, not to mention privacy.

The sticky command hooks are the perfect item you need! All you have to do is

Need a temporary curtain to create separation in your RV, don't want to drill holes into the frame, or simply want a super easy way to hang curtains. Use command hooks to hold up your curtain rod! Command hooks, or something similar has the perfect spacing for a small rod. And they peel right off when you don't want curtains anymore!

They are also great to hang Christmas lights and decorations for a festive fun holiday!

RV/Camping Hack #2

Camping and RV'ing is a lot of fun. But that fun turns quickly south when there's too many pesky flies to shoo away!

Did you know that you can use Pin Sol to keep them away? Yes!

Dilute it with water to create a 50/50 solution and wipe down your counters, tables, and awnings with it. You'll love the enjoyment this little hack gives you freedom from the pesky bugs.

EGG IN A BASKET

INGREDIENTS
  1 slice of bread
  1 egg
  2 pieces bacon or ham

DIRECTIONS
  Brown meat in a skillet.
  Tear a hole out of the middle of the bread slice (approx. 1 1/2 in diameter).
  Place the bread slice on top of the strips of meat.
  Carefully break the egg into the hole in the bread.
  Cook until the egg is the desired firmness.

BAG KABOBS

INGREDIENTS
 beef or chicken
 1 bell peppers
 mushrooms
 1 onion
 10 small potatoes
 1 zucchini squash
 2-3 Tbsp olive oil
 1 lemon or lime
 McCormick's Salt-free Chicken seasoning
 powdered butter flavoring
 2 Tbsp soy sauce
 lemon pepper seasonings
 dill

DIRECTIONS

Boil potatoes for approximately 4-5 minutes depending on size.

They should still be firm and crisp, not mushy. They will finish cooking on the grill. Let potatoes cool completely before putting in foil bag. Chop bell peppers, onion and zucchini squash into large pieces.

Put chopped vegetables, whole potatoes and whole mushrooms into a large foil bag, olive oil, lemon or lime juice, soy sauce, butter flavoring, lemon pepper seasonings, and dill.

Cut meat into large stew size pieces.

Put meat in a separate foil bag with 1/4 cup of olive oil, garlic, chicken seasonings, butter flavoring and 2 tablespoons of soy sauce.

BAG KABOBS

When using more than one kind of meat, put in separate bags. Place the foil bags into larger 2 gallon zip lock bags to store while traveling.

To cook, remove foil bags from plastic zip lock bags and grill for 8-10 minutes, turning after 5-6 minutes.

Let sit before opening bags.

APPLES ON A STICK

Apple pie anytime is amazing. But apple pie on a stick…that's just taking it to a whole new level! This is a fun and tasty treat any camper is sure to enjoy.

INGREDIENTS
- 1 c sugar
- 1 Tbsp cinnamon
- 4 cooking apples
- 4 dowel or roasting sticks

DIRECTIONS

In a small bowl, mix together sugar and cinnamon and set aside.

Push the stick or dowel through the top of the apple to the bottom until the apple is secure.

Roast the apple 2 to 3 inches above the bed of hot coals and turn frequently. As the apple cooks, the skin starts to brown and the juice dribbles out.

When the skin is loose, remove the apple from the coals but leave it on the stick. Peel the skin off the apple, being careful not to burn yourself because the apple is very hot.

CANDY CANE DONUTS

MAKES 6 SERVINGS

Ingredients
Donuts
1 1/4 cups moist-style devil's food cake mix (a little less than half a box)
1/2 cup canned pure pumpkin
1/4 cup (about 2 large) egg whites or fat-free liquid egg substitute
1/4 tsp. peppermint extract

Glaze
1/2 cup powdered sugar
1 1/2 tbsp. unsweetened vanilla almond milk, light vanilla soymilk, or fat-free dairy milk
2 - 3 drops peppermint extract
Dash salt
1 full-sized candy cane (or 3 minis), crushed

DIRECTIONS

Preheat oven to 400 degrees. Spray a 6-cavity standard donut pan with nonstick spray.

In a large bowl, combine all donut ingredients. Add 1/4 cup water, and mix until completely smooth and uniform. Evenly distribute batter into the rings of the donut pan, and smooth out the tops. (See HG Tip below.)

Bake until a toothpick inserted into a donut comes out mostly clean, about 12 minutes.

Meanwhile, place a cooling rack over a baking sheet.

Let donuts cool completely, about 10 minutes in the pan and 15 minutes on the cooling rack.

In a medium bowl, combine glaze ingredients *except* candy cane, and whisk until smooth and uniform.

One at a time, dunk the tops of the donuts into the glaze, coating the top halves. Return to the cooling rack, and sprinkle evenly with crushed candy cane.

Allow glaze to set, about 10 minutes. (Glaze will run off; that's why you've got the rack over that baking sheet.)

If you enjoyed reading this book as much as I enjoyed writing it then be sure to return to the Amazon page and leave a review.

Go to Tonyakappes.com for a full reading order of my novels and while there join my newsletter. You can also find links to Facebook, Instagram and Goodreads.

Join like-minded readers like YOU in the Cozy Krew Facebook Group for dream casting, fan theories, and live Q & A's. It's like a BIG GIANT BOOK CLUB! But if you want to have your own book club, be sure you let me know! I love to send goodies.

Christmas, Criminals, & Campers
Book Club Questions

1. Tonight we are discussing Christmas, Criminals, and Campers, Book 4 of the Campers & Criminals Cozy Mystery Series.
   Was this your first trip to Normal, Kentucky?

2. Have you ever had the opportunity to meet your book idol? Did you go all fan girl/guy or did you keep it cool? How was the experience?

3. Are you a fan of camping, or in today's world, glamping?

4. Mae hasn't had the easiest life. She is quite upset when her adoptive mother shows up for the holidays. Did you think she overreacted with her anger?

5. When Mae and Hank go on their first real date. How did this make you feel? Do you see a future for these two?

6. "When Abby was suspected of murder, Mae was going to make sure her friend was not going to get convicted. When Mary Elizabeth wanted to help, did this surprise you? How would you feel solving a crime with your mom or family member?

7. Mary Elizabeth passed a large olive branch to Mae, her prized pearls. I am a huge fan of pearls, just so classic. Do you have a piece of jewelry or an heirloom that a family member has passed down to you?

8. When Dawn came in to Normal so fast from Chicago, did you suspect her? Did it ever seem slightly shady she was in Normal the day before and lied to Mae?

9. When you found out who the killer/killers were, how did that make you feel? Was it a fun surprise?

A NOTE FROM TONYA

Thank y'all so much for this amazing journey we've been on with all the fun cozy mystery adventures! We've had so much fun and I can't wait to bring you a lot more of them. When I set out to write about them, I pulled from my experiences from camping, having a camper, and fond memories of camping.

Readers ask me if there's a real place like those in my books. Sadly, no. It's a combination of places I've stayed and would own if I could.

XOXO ~ Tonya

For a full reading order of Tonya Kappes's Novels, visit Tonyakappes.com

Also By Tonya Kappes

A Camper and Criminals Cozy Mystery
BEACHES, BUNGALOWS, & BURGLARIES
DESERTS, DRIVERS, & DERELICTS
FORESTS, FISHING, & FORGERY
CHRISTMAS, CRIMINALS, & CAMPERS
MOTORHOMES, MAPS, & MURDER
CANYONS, CARAVANS, & CADAVERS
HITCHES, HIDEOUTS, & HOMICIDE
ASSAILANTS, ASPHALT, & ALIBIS
VALLEYS, VEHICLES & VICTIMS
SUNSETS, SABBATICAL, & SCANDAL
TENTS, TRAILS, & TURMOIL
KICKBACKS, KAYAKS, & KIDNAPPING
GEAR, GRILLS, & GUNS
EGGNOG, EXTORTION, & EVERGREENS
ROPES, RIDDLES, & ROBBERIES
PADDLERS, PROMISES, & POISON
INSECTS, IVY, & INVESTIGATIONS
OUTDOORS, OARS, & OATHS
WILDLIFE, WARRANTS, & WEAPONS
BLOSSOMS, BARBEQUE, & BLACKMAIL
LANTERNS, LAKES, & LARCENY
JACKETS, JACK-O-LANTERN, & JUSTICE
SANTA, SUNRISES, & SUSPICIONS
VISTAS, VICES, & VALENTINES
ADVENTURE, ABDUCTION, & ARREST
RANGERS, RV'S, & REVENGE
CAMPFIRES, COURAGE, & CONVICTS
TRAPPING, TURKEYS, & THANKSGIVING
GIFTS, GLAMPING, & GLOCKS

ALSO BY TONYA KAPPES

Kenni Lowry Mystery Series
FIXIN' TO DIE
SOUTHERN FRIED
AX TO GRIND
SIX FEET UNDER
DEAD AS A DOORNAIL
TANGLED UP IN TINSEL
DIGGIN' UP DIRT
BLOWIN' UP A MURDER

Killer Coffee Mystery Series
SCENE OF THE GRIND
MOCHA AND MURDER
FRESHLY GROUND MURDER
COLD BLOODED BREW
DECAFFEINATED SCANDAL
A KILLER LATTE
HOLIDAY ROAST MORTEM
DEAD TO THE LAST DROP
A CHARMING BLEND NOVELLA (CROSSOVER WITH MAGICAL CURES MYSTERY)
FROTHY FOUL PLAY
SPOONFUL OF MURDER
BARISTA BUMP-OFF

Holiday Cozy Mystery
FOUR LEAF FELONY
MOTHER'S DAY MURDER
A HALLOWEEN HOMICIDE
CHOCOLATE BUNNY BETRAYAL
APRIL FOOL'S ALIBI
Father's Day MURDER
THANKSGIVING TREACHERY

ALSO BY TONYA KAPPES

SANTA CLAUSE SURPRISE
NEW YEAR NUISANCE

Mail Carrier Cozy Mystery
STAMPED OUT
ADDRESS FOR MURDER
ALL SHE WROTE
RETURN TO SENDER
FIRST CLASS KILLER
POST MORTEM
DEADLY DELIVERY
RED LETTER SLAY

Magical Cures Mystery Series
A CHARMING CRIME
A CHARMING CURE
A CHARMING POTION (novella)
A CHARMING WISH
A CHARMING SPELL
A CHARMING MAGIC
A CHARMING SECRET
A CHARMING CHRISTMAS (novella)
A CHARMING FATALITY
A CHARMING DEATH (novella)
A CHARMING GHOST
A CHARMING HEX
A CHARMING VOODOO
A CHARMING CORPSE
A CHARMING MISFORTUNE
A CHARMING BLEND (CROSSOVER WITH A KILLER COFFEE COZY)
A CHARMING DECEPTION

ALSO BY TONYA KAPPES

A Southern Magical Bakery Cozy Mystery Serial
A SOUTHERN MAGICAL BAKERY

A Ghostly Southern Mystery Series
A GHOSTLY UNDERTAKING
A GHOSTLY GRAVE
A GHOSTLY DEMISE
A GHOSTLY MURDER
A GHOSTLY REUNION
A GHOSTLY MORTALITY
A GHOSTLY SECRET
A GHOSTLY SUSPECT

A Southern Cake Baker Series
(WRITTEN UNDER MAYEE BELL)
CAKE AND PUNISHMENT
BATTER OFF DEAD

Spies and Spells Mystery Series
SPIES AND SPELLS
BETTING OFF DEAD
GET WITCH or DIE TRYING

A Laurel London Mystery Series
CHECKERED CRIME
CHECKERED PAST
CHECKERED THIEF

A Divorced Diva Beading Mystery Series
A BEAD OF DOUBT SHORT STORY
STRUNG OUT TO DIE
CRIMPED TO DEATH

ALSO BY TONYA KAPPES

Olivia Davis Paranormal Mystery Series
SPLITSVILLE.COM
COLOR ME LOVE (novella)
COLOR ME A CRIME

About Tonya

Tonya has written over 100 novels, all of which have graced numerous bestseller lists, including the USA Today. Best known for stories charged with emotion and humor and filled with flawed characters, her novels have garnered reader praise and glowing critical reviews. She lives with her husband and a very spoiled rescue cat named Ro. Tonya grew up in the small southern Kentucky town of Nicholasville. Now that her four boys are grown men, Tonya writes full-time in her camper she calls her SHAMPER (she-camper).

Learn more about her be sure to check out her website tonyakappes.com. Find her on Facebook, Twitter, BookBub, and Instagram

Sign up to receive her newsletter, where you'll get free books, exclusive bonus content, and news of her releases and sales.

If you liked this book, please take a few minutes to leave a review now! Authors (Tonya included) really appreciate this, and it helps draw more readers to books they might like. Thanks!

Cover artist: Mariah Sinclair: The Cover Vault

This book is a work of fiction. The characters, incidents, and dialogue are drawn from the author's imagination and are not to be construed as real. Any resemblance to actual events or persons, living or dead, is entirely coincidental. The cover was made by Mariah Sinclair.

Copyright © 2018 by Tonya Kappes. All rights reserved. Printed in the United States of America. No part of this book may be used or reproduced in any manner whatsoever without written permission except in the case of brief quotations embodied in critical articles and reviews. For information email Tonyakappes@tonyakappes.com

Lightning Source UK Ltd.
Milton Keynes UK
UKHW022215191022
410752UK00010B/680